W9-AUX-883

The Trap

Nancy Rue

BETHANY HOUSE PUBLISHERS
MINNEAPOLIS, MINNESOTA 55438

Published by Bethany House Publishers
A Ministry of Bethany Fellowship International
11300 Hampshire Avenue South
Minneapolis, Minnesota 55438

Printed in the United States of America by
Bethany Press International, Minneapolis, Minnesota 55438

Library of Congress Cataloging-in-Publication Data

Rue, Nancy N.
    The trap / Nancy Rue
        p. cm. — (The Christian heritage series, the Charleston years ; bk. 4)
    Summary: Having become embroiled in one troublesome situation after another while living on his uncle's plantation in South Carolina in 1861, eleven-year-old Austin eventually accuses his older relative of hypocrisy.
    ISBN 1–56179–567–4
[1. Family life—South Carolina—Fiction. 2. Hypocrisy—Fiction.
3. Slavery—Fiction. 4. South Carolina—Fiction.]
I. Title. II. Series: Rue, Nancy N. Christian heritage series, the Charleston years ; bk. 4.
PZ7.R88515Tr   1998
[Fic]—dc21   97–51660
                                                        CIP
                                                         AC

---

98 99 00 01 02 03 04 / 12 11 10 9 8 7 6 5 4 3 2 1

For Temple Garnett,

who like Lottie is a gentle daughter of the South

Canaan Grove Plantation,
Charleston
1860-1861

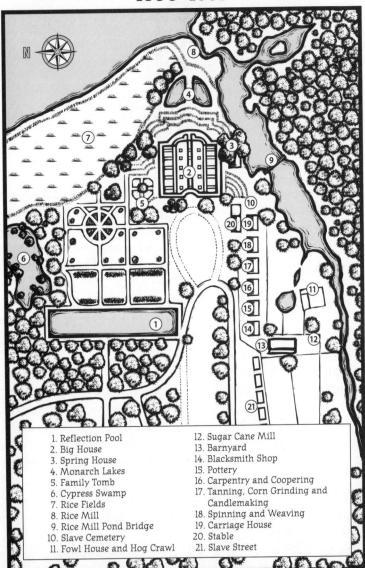

1. Reflection Pool
2. Big House
3. Spring House
4. Monarch Lakes
5. Family Tomb
6. Cypress Swamp
7. Rice Fields
8. Rice Mill
9. Rice Mill Pond Bridge
10. Slave Cemetery
11. Fowl House and Hog Crawl
12. Sugar Cane Mill
13. Barnyard
14. Blacksmith Shop
15. Pottery
16. Carpentry and Coopering
17. Tanning, Corn Grinding and Candlemaking
18. Spinning and Weaving
19. Carriage House
20. Stable
21. Slave Street

"Massa Austin, what you doin'? Get your white self down from there 'fore all the blood rush to your head!"

Austin lifted his head of deer-colored hair from its upside-down position in the oak tree and grinned down at his slave friend.

"I'm doing a scientific experiment, Henry-James," he said.

Thirteen-year-old Henry-James arched a dark eyebrow. "You tryin' to find out how long a boy can hang by his knees from a tree 'fore he faint dead away?"

Austin grinned again—and wondered how a smile looked upside down. "No," he said, pulling himself upright on the branch by his lanky arms. "I wanted to see how gravity looks backward. You know, if I dropped something, would it go up or down?"

From below him on the picnic cloth, three faces looked at him blankly. Bogie, Henry-James's blood-houndish mutt, shook his big, floppy-skinned head.

"What you talkin' 'bout, Massa Austin?" Henry-James said. "I don't know nothin' 'bout no gravity."

"What *is* gravity, Boston Austin?"

Austin dropped down beside 11-year-old Charlotte. She was

1

cocking her head—with its hair the same color as his—and surveying him out of her quiet, golden-brown eyes, also the same color as his. In fact, almost everything about them was so much alike, they looked more like twins than cousins. The only difference was that Charlotte's hair cascaded over her shoulders, while Austin's was close-cropped around his ears and formed a wispy fringe across his forehead.

"I read a book about it," Austin said.

"Now tell me somethin', Massa Austin," Henry-James said. "Is there anything you *ain't* read a book about?"

Austin had to stop and think about that, which he did while pulling the last of the peppermint cakes out of the picnic basket. His little brother Jefferson's pudgy face pinched into a frown.

"Why do we gotta talk about gravididdy? We're supposed to be havin' a picnic."

"We're having it," Austin said, shoving most of the cake into his mouth.

Charlotte stretched out on the grass beside the cloth and tapped the toes of her high-topped, button-up shoes together. "This could be the last chance we have for a picnic," she said. "It's going to start getting cold soon."

"This been my *first* chance," Henry-James said.

"You've been working too hard," Austin said. "Doing all that harvesting and threshing, plus being Uncle Drayton's body slave."

"All that harvestin' and threshin' done now," Henry-James said. "And I thank the Lord for that."

Austin did, too. Ever since they had all come back from their summer in Flat Rock, North Carolina, he'd spent a lot of time watching Henry-James work. It was Henry-James's first year out in the fields, but he'd kept up with the best of them, standing shoulder high among the rice plants, harvesting the grain with a sickle-shaped rice hook, and putting it out to dry.

Austin, Charlotte, and Jefferson had perched in the trees for days, watching the slaves and the poor whites Uncle Drayton had hired to help tie the dried grain into sheaves and stack it on the flat boats to be taken to the threshing and pounding mill.

"Daddy 'Lias say *he* thank the Lord that Marse Drayton finally done got hisself a mill," Henry-James said now. "They used to like to kill theyselves doin' that all by the strength of they arms and the sweat of they brows."

For weeks they'd listened to the huge millstones rotate and the heavy pestles pound. Austin couldn't picture Henry-James and the others, men and women alike, doing all of that by hand, although Aunt Olivia had complained endlessly of a headache and said it was so much quieter the old way.

"But this brings in the money so much faster, my dear," Uncle Drayton had said to her with his usual charming smile. "You just think about that new French Victorian furniture that's on its way." His golden-brown eyes had twinkled. "That should cure your headache."

As far as Austin was concerned, Aunt Olivia *was* a headache.

"So what are we going to do now?" Jefferson said, peering into the empty picnic basket. "I'm bored."

"I could give you all a science lesson," Austin said. "Do you know what the name of that tree is?"

"The one you was just danglin' from?" Henry-James said.

"That's a live oak, Boston," Charlotte said.

"Nope, it's a *Quercus virginiana.*"

Henry-James fingered the gap between his two front teeth. "I done lived at Canaan Grove all my life, Massa Austin, and I ain't never heard of no tree called no 'quirkus Virginia.' This here is South Carolina!"

"That's the Latin name," Austin said. "That butternut hickory over there? That's a *Carya cordipormis.*"

"Carry a what?" Jefferson said.

"Now let me ask you somethin', Massa Austin," Henry-James

said. "What good them big fancy words gonna do you? I mean, besides makin' you sound smart, which we already knows you is anyway."

Austin shrugged happily. "I don't know. I just like knowing things. And you can never tell when a piece of information might come in handy. Like, I've been reading about inventions—you know, the cotton gin and the sewing machine and the steam engine. All of them came from knowing simple science."

"You sayin' by knowin' that there hickory tree be a carry-a-corpse, you could make you an invention, Massa Austin?"

"You talk about *me* being smart!" Austin said. "You almost got it, Henry-James! It's *Carya cordipormis*—"

"I don't care about that!" Jefferson said, flouncing himself around. "I want to do something *fun!*"

Since Jefferson's idea of fun usually involved cornering a skunk or dumping a bucket of water over someone's head, Austin quickly scrambled for an idea. Before he got even a glimmer of one, Charlotte groaned, and Bogie lifted his big head and sniffed warily.

"What's wrong, Miz Lottie?" Henry-James asked.

Charlotte pointed across the lawn, where two figures were hurrying from the direction of the spring house toward the big plantation mansion. It was 17-year-old Kady, being held by the arm by her mother, Austin's Aunt Olivia, who as usual was wagging her elaborately piled head of dark hair while she scolded away. They could hear it even from there.

"Mr. Garrison McCloud is waiting in our parlor, and here you are dressed like a schoolmarm!"

"I *am* a schoolmarm, Mama!"

"You are nothing of the kind, and don't you dare tell Mr. McCloud that you are teaching our slaves to read! We are outsiders enough these days!"

Austin watched thoughtfully as they disappeared up the back

steps and inside the Big House. "Who's Garrison McCloud?" he said.

"He's another beau Mama and Daddy lined up for Kady," Charlotte said. "She already met him at the Singletons' barbecue."

"Does he like him?" Austin asked.

"No, she says he's boring."

"I know about boring!" Jefferson said impatiently.

Charlotte's eyes began to sparkle. "But Polly likes him. That's all she talked about when we came home. 'Garrison smiled at me. . . . Garrison picked up my handkerchief.' "

Austin snorted. "Probably only because she threw it right on his toes!"

"Speakin' of the devil," Henry-James muttered.

Austin looked up and snorted again. Fourteen-year-old Polly was that very moment emerging from the back door, dressed in yellow with enough bows and lace and ribbons to clothe three girls. Her skirt swayed on its wide hoop so that only the dainty toes of her yellow shoes peeked out. Polly herself peeked out from under a wide-brimmed straw hat. Austin studied her carefully as she swept down the steps and paraded across the lawn.

"There's something different about her," he said.

"She ain't got Tot with her," Henry-James said.

That was true. It was odd to see Polly without her stump-shaped slave girl.

"That's because she wants to flirt with Kady's beau," Charlotte said, wrinkling her freckled nose. "Which I think is disgusting. But if she's going to do it, she can't have Tot around. She's likely to trip the boy!"

Austin shook his head. "But that isn't what's different about her. I think she looks . . . I don't know, *better*."

It was Charlotte's turn to snort. "She couldn't have looked worse!"

That was probably true, too. Poor Polly. Limp, brass-colored hair hung at her neck like wilted stems, refusing to go into curls no matter how many hours she made Tot work at it. Her eyes weren't quite brown and weren't quite green, so they blinked in the mire somewhere in between. Her too-skinny arms and legs always seemed to be flying out in four opposite directions. And worst of all, she had brown teeth. It was no wonder she didn't smile very much.

Austin's mother, Sally Hutchinson, said Polly was an almost-there version of her father, who was really quite handsome. "She'll grow into herself," Mother said whenever the topic came up. "Drayton was no beauty when he was that age, and neither was I. You just give her time."

"And prayer," Kady always added.

It wasn't surprising that Kady and Charlotte didn't give Polly much room. She'd always been her mother's pet, which meant she tattled on her sisters every chance she got. When Austin had first arrived last January, Polly had started in on him like he was a tiger's fresh meat—although he had to admit that he hadn't missed many chances to get back at her. But last summer, they'd called a truce, and she had started being nicer . . . at least as nice as Polly could be.

"That there must be Massa McCloud," Henry-James said.

They all looked toward the back door where Kady was stepping out, still in her gray-and-black striped dress with a net over her thick, dark hair. A young man barely an inch taller than she came out behind her. His hair was so blond that it was nearly blinding. He ran his hand carefully over it, perched his pearl-gray hat jauntily on it, and smoothed his waistcoat over his broad chest.

Bogie gave a low growl.

"You don't like that boy, Bogie?" Charlotte said, giggling.

"Ain't nobody good enough for Miz Kady, far as we sees it,"

Henry-James said. He breathed in until his nostrils flared. "If'n she don't like him, I hopes Marse Drayton don't make her marry him."

"*Make* her?" Austin said, twisting to look at Henry-James. "He wouldn't do that, would he?"

"He wouldn't have to force Polly," Charlotte said, pointing. "Look at that!"

Polly swirled around on the path toward the gardens and put her hand over her mouth. "Oh my, Kady!" she sang out. "I didn't see you there. Oh, and Mr. *McCloud!*"

" 'Mr. McCloud!' " Charlotte mocked her in a high-pitched voice. "Oh, please."

Garrison McCloud smiled an immediate smile and held out his free arm to Polly. The three of them strolled off into the gardens and disappeared amid the crepe myrtles.

"At least he didn't chase Polly off like Kady's last beau did," Austin said.

"That was funny!" Charlotte said. "She didn't speak to Kady for days—which didn't bother Kady!"

"I'm still bored!" Jefferson said with a squall.

"You won't be bored tomorrow at the corn-husking party, Jefferson," Charlotte said. "Think about that."

"I don't even know what a corn-husking party is," Jefferson said. He folded his arms stubbornly across his chest.

"It's one of the best times of the whole year!" Charlotte said. "There's more food than you can even think about, and games and the husking, of course, which is fun."

"And don't be forgettin' 'bout the wrestlin'," Henry-James put in.

"Wrestling?" Austin said.

"There's a big wrestling match to see who's the best on the plantation," Charlotte said. She grinned at Henry-James. "This is your first year!"

Henry-James nodded his woolly head and gave one of his rare smiles. "I been practicin' with Isaac and them."

"Isaac's the biggest slave at Canaan Grove!" Austin said. "Didn't he hurt you?"

"He just showin' me some tricks. We ain't gon' fight together. I be wrestlin' other boys same size as me."

"Like me," said a voice behind them.

They all turned to see a dark-haired boy leaning, cross-armed, against a palm tree several yards away. Austin had seen him before, working in Uncle Drayton's fields with his father and brother. He'd thought then as he thought now: *This boy has the tightest looking mouth I ever saw! It looks like a line across his face.*

He also had a big head with one sliver of hair that wouldn't join the rest of his combed-back thatch and fell down over his high forehead. He stared at them now with bright green eyes.

Henry-James stared back for a minute and then lowered his gaze, the way he'd been taught to do around white folks—except Charlotte, Kady, Jefferson, and Austin, who considered him a friend. Charlotte, too, looked down at the picnic cloth. She always did that around people she didn't know . . . or didn't like.

That left Austin to do the talking. It was a job he didn't mind much.

"I'm Austin Hutchinson," he said. "And you are—?"

The green eyes pointed like darts. "You ain't from around here," the boy said.

Austin grinned. "Oh, you mean my accent. I'm from up north. My mother and my brother and I are staying here for a while because my father travels and my mother was too sick to go with him."

"A Yankee," the boy said. His mouth tightened so hard that Austin looked closely to see how he was going to talk out of it. "I don't like Yankees," he muttered from the slit.

"Then I'm glad you're not going to wrestle *me*," Austin said cheerfully. "Now Henry-James is a native South Carolinian, born right here in St. Paul's Parish—"

"I don't like darkies either."

"Then I don't like *you!*" Jefferson cried, getting up on his knees and doubling his pudgy fists. His blue eyes were blazing.

The boy ignored him and fixed his own green ones on Henry-James. "How 'bout you and me fight right now?" he said.

Charlotte looked up sharply, but Henry-James still stared at his knees.

Austin felt the first poking of irritation in his backbone. "It's all right, Henry-James," he said. "You can look at him. He's a worker, same as you."

"I ain't the same as him!" the boy shrieked. "I ain't one bit the same as him!"

And then he charged the picnic blanket and hurled himself onto Henry-James.

Charlotte cried out and scrambled up, dragging Jefferson with her. Austin crawled over to the struggling pair, shouting, "That isn't fair! You took him by surprise!"

His answer was an elbow in the face that knocked him backward and sent him rolling off the blanket.

"Stop!" Charlotte screamed. "Austin, make them stop!"

But Austin didn't even know where to start. With fists flying and legs wrapped around other legs, it was hard to tell where Henry-James left off and the white boy began.

Bogie seemed to know, though. With a juicy snarl, he hurled himself into the fray and chomped his teeth down on the boy's plaid shirt. Digging his front paws into the ground and poking his backside in the air, Bogie tugged, still growling. But the white boy didn't so much as slow down, even when his shirt ripped and Bogie tumbled backward.

"He's going to hurt Henry-James!" Charlotte cried. "He's going to kill him!"

But just then Henry-James emerged on top of the rolling pile of arms and legs and pinned the white boy flat on his back. He held his shoulders with both of his square hands and breathed down on him, nostrils flaring in and out like a blacksmith's bellows.

"Get him, Henry-James!" Jefferson shouted.

"Don't you do anything of the kind, boy!" a voice behind them trumpeted. "Or you will have me to reckon with!"

Chapter Two

ncle Drayton's eyes were like two gas flames as he glared down at Henry-James and the white boy. Austin knew right away why. Uncle Drayton had company—bad company.

There were three men with him, and Austin recognized two of them. They were Virgil Rhett and Lawson Chesnut, two of the people Uncle Drayton called Fire Eaters, because they were ready any moment to break South Carolina away from the Union. Austin had run into them several times, and every time they opened their mouths, it was as if fire were spewing out.

"My, my, Mr. Ravenal," said Lawson Chesnut, rubbing his thick face where his side whiskers met his mustache. "It looks as if you have lost control over your property."

Henry-James isn't property, Austin thought angrily. But he knew better than to say anything. Uncle Drayton might not believe in secession, but he still believed in slavery, and slaves were as much belongings as the furniture.

By now Henry-James had peeled himself off the white boy and was cowering, head down, at the edge of the picnic blanket. The white boy took off like a spooked cat with Bogie snapping at his heels. Charlotte looked like she wanted to flee, too, but Austin knew she wouldn't leave Henry-James when he was in trouble. And neither would Austin.

"Sir," Austin said, "I just want you to know that the white boy, whatever his name is, jumped Henry-James first!"

But Uncle Drayton, his face severe, was looking at Henry-James. "What do you mean, fighting a white boy?" he said.

"I's sorry, Marse Drayton," Henry James said meekly.

"Sorry!" Austin cried. "There wasn't anything else he could do!"

"He could have refused to strike back, as he has been taught to do."

"He would have been killed!"

"Austin, enough!" Uncle Drayton snapped.

"You still bein' troubled with this boy?" Virgil Rhett said, pointing to Henry-James. His bushy eyebrows crawled together like two caterpillars. "I'd have gotten rid of him long ago!" He turned to mutter something to the other man, the one Austin didn't recognize, with the funny-shaped head that almost came to a point.

"Off with you now, boy!" Uncle Drayton said to Henry-James. "I shall deal with you later!"

"Don't put off the whippin' on our account, Ravenal," Lawson Chesnut said, practically licking his chops.

Uncle Drayton almost never whips his slaves, Austin wanted to say. But Charlotte seemed to read his mind, and she yanked him over to stand beside her as Henry-James ran off toward Slave Street.

"So much for his afternoon off," Austin muttered.

"Now then, Mr. Ravenal," the third man said, working his eyebrows up and down. "As I was sayin' before this ruckus began, we are countin' on you to change your mind on this secession issue."

"No, Mr. Yancey," Uncle Drayton said, "I think *I* was saying that you might just as well save your breath. I am not yet ready for the South to secede from the Union. Not as long as there is still a chance for us to remain united."

"There is no chance!" Yancey said. He looked as if he smelled something bad. "As soon as Abraham Lincoln is elected, slavery will be over and our way of life will be extinguished like a candle."

"We must fight Lincoln!" Virgil Rhett broke in. "It's like my cousin, the great William Rhett, says, 'Liberty and the Spirit of 1776!' "

"If Mr. Lincoln *is* elected," Uncle Drayton said, "he is not the extremist you have made him out to be. He has already said that he will do nothing to disturb slavery in the South—"

Austin cleared his throat. "Actually, sir, I read that Mr. Lincoln thinks slavery will eventually disappear on its own."

"You see!" Yancey cried. The other two men bobbed their heads angrily. "Lincoln is a radical! We have everything to fear from his election . . . unless we break away."

Uncle Drayton pulled his glaring eyes away from Austin. "I have always respected the thinking of Jefferson Davis in making my decisions, and he is no secessionist."

"Jeff Davis is lukewarm!" Rhett shouted.

"And you would prefer a hothead like yourself?" Uncle Drayton said.

Austin could tell he was having trouble not shouting.

"I call it passion," Yancey said. "I only wish you had some of it. We need to be of one mind here in the South."

"I am of one mind—my own." Uncle Drayton riveted his eyes on Virgil Rhett, whose eyebrows had become hopelessly tangled. "I trust I may think as I please without fear of injury to myself and my family. That *is* what was decided this last summer in Flat Rock."

Austin remembered that Virgil Rhett hadn't been happy about that decision. He watched carefully as Rhett reluctantly nodded.

"Now," Uncle Drayton went on, "if the South weren't running

wild with people who are eaten up with their passion, we might have a chance to remain in the Union and hold on to our majority in Congress and our control of the Supreme Court."

"But we will always be under the control of those villainous Yankees. They'll see to that." Yancey glowered at Austin as if he himself were responsible for the entire North. "It goes against my personal honor to even be in the presence of a Yankee."

"Then your honor is rather thin, Yancey," Uncle Drayton said, "if that is all it takes to threaten it."

"I have fought three duels in defense of my honor!" said Yancey.

Uncle Drayton shook his deer-colored head. "Then you're even more of a fool than I thought."

It was as if Uncle Drayton had fired a cannon at them. All three of the Fire Eaters bolted across the lawn to their carriage in the drive, spitting sparks of outrage.

Charlotte tugged on Austin's arm. "Let's go," she whispered, "before Daddy yells at you."

Austin grabbed Jefferson's hand and followed her at a scamper. Uncle Drayton's bugling voice stopped them at the second step.

"If you are going anywhere," he said, "get yourselves to Slave Street and tell that boy he had better be in my bedroom laying my fire before supper."

Austin couldn't keep his teeth clamped down on his tongue any longer. "You aren't going to whip him, are you?"

He could hear Charlotte groaning beside him.

"No," Uncle Drayton said. "But he is back on thin ice. If he wants to continue to train as my body slave, he'd better be careful."

He stalked off on his long, lean legs toward the Big House, and Charlotte hauled Austin on toward Slave Street. Jefferson raced ahead.

"That really isn't true, you know," Austin said. "What your father just said about Henry-James being about to lose his place as his body slave. He told Henry-James last summer he was the best one he's ever had."

"I just think your mouth is going to get you into trouble one of these days, Austin," Charlotte said. "It scares me when you say some of the things you do to Daddy."

Austin shrugged. "*My* father taught me to speak my mind and ask questions."

"But *your* daddy isn't here, is he?"

Austin felt a stab deep inside. No, his father wasn't there, and every day it was a little harder to be away from him. The only reason he didn't beg his mother to take them back to the North now that she was feeling so much better was because he loved the plantation and his friends almost as much as he loved his father.

But as always, the sight of the slave cabin Henry-James shared with his mother, Ria, and his grandfather, Daddy Elias, chased all sad thoughts out of his head. The sagging porch, the glassless windows, the straggly vegetable garden—they welcomed him like a hug.

Daddy Elias and Henry-James were inside, out of the gathering chill. There was a small fire crackling in the fireplace, and Daddy Elias sat in his rocking chair, soaking his feet in a wooden bucket.

"What's that?" Austin said as Jefferson scrambled into his customary place on the old man's lap.

"That there is white oak bark in warm water," Daddy Elias said in his crackly voice. "Ria done whipped that up for me 'fore she left to look after your mama. She say it's good for achin' feet."

"She must be the best doctor in the South," Austin said, settling himself on the worn rug. "Ever since she started taking care of my mother, she's like a whole different person. She goes outside every day. It used to be she never got out of bed."

"Daddy sent us to tell you to come lay his fire before supper," Charlotte said to Henry-James. "And he said you're not going to get a whipping. You're just supposed to be careful or he won't let you be his body slave anymore. Only Austin says he doesn't believe that—"

But Henry-James didn't wait to hear why. He rushed out of the cabin, and they could hear his bare feet beating on the sandy path outside.

Daddy Elias sighed. "Look like I's gon' have to fix my own supper again."

"What are you having?" said a voice from the doorway. "I can cook it."

Austin didn't know which surprised him more, the fact that it was Polly at the door or that she was volunteering to make supper. Actually, she'd come to the cabin with the children several times since they'd gotten back from Flat Rock, but she'd never looked so pleased about it as she did now. Her face was pink and glowing, and she was smiling. Again, Austin studied her to see what was so different about her all of a sudden.

Tot was with her, of course, stumbling heavily into the room. Charlotte looked at her doubtfully.

"You aren't going to get near the fireplace, are you, Tot?" she said. "You know what always happens with you and fire."

Tot gave her head a confused shake, but Polly tossed hers confidently. "I am going to do the cooking," she said. "I've been spending a lot of time with Josephine in the cook house. It's time I learned my way around a kitchen."

"We know," Charlotte said with a moan. "You're going to be a wife someday."

"But if you marry a rich man, you'll have slaves to do that," Austin said.

Polly picked up a piece of cloth from the back of a kitchen chair and tied it around the waist of her dark brown dress. "Some men like a woman who can cook for the family if she has to," she said.

"Some men?" Charlotte said slyly. "You mean, Garrison McCloud? *Kady's* beau?"

She grinned devilishly at Austin.

"So what can you cook, Polly?" he said.

"Everything," she said, with Tot nodding 10 times in agreement. "What are you having tonight, Daddy Elias?"

"I was fixin' to have me some collards and peas, with some cornbread and milk, and maybe a little rice."

"Oh," Polly said, face flushing. "I don't know how to make that yet."

"I do," Charlotte said. "I've watched Ria do it before." She headed for the table and Polly followed, looking a little unsure of herself.

"You boil the rice with the vegetables till the rice is done," Charlotte said to her. "Do you have any salt pork to put in, Daddy 'Lias?"

Daddy Elias pointed to the slice of bacon hanging from the ceiling and turned to Jefferson. "Now Massa Jefferson, case you gets hungry smellin' all this cookin', you better get you a lump of brown sugar from that there barrel."

"No!" Austin said. "There won't be enough for Henry-James!"

"What we got, you all is welcome to," Daddy Elias said. "That be how the good Lord want it."

And if the good Lord wanted it, that was the way it should be. Austin had learned that in his 10 months at Canaan Grove. But something about that bothered him at the moment.

"I don't think Uncle Drayton is good friends with Jesus the way we are," he said to Daddy Elias.

Daddy Elias drew in his spoon-shaped mouth and rubbed a crusty hand across his forehead. It wrinkled all the way up to his snow-white cap of hair. "What drive you to say that, Massa Austin?"

"Last summer I told him what you taught me—you know, about always putting Jesus first and then you'll know what to do. He said that helped him, but I think he forgot it."

Daddy Elias just swished his feet in the bucket and rocked.

"Just today," Austin went on, "he told Henry-James he should have let some white boy beat him up, just because the boy's white and Henry-James is black. I don't think Jesus would do that."

"Speaking of Jesus," Jefferson said, straightening tall on Daddy Elias's knees, "tell us a Jesus story, Daddy 'Lias. I'm tired of Austin talking."

"But what about—?" Austin started to say.

Daddy Elias smiled at him and winked one of his crinkly old eyes. "I reckon I got a story just perfect for right now."

"Tell it, then," Jefferson said and squirmed into a comfortable position.

Austin sighed impatiently, but he stretched out on the rug. A Jesus story from Daddy Elias was the next best thing to getting the answer he needed.

"Now," Daddy Elias said, "once upon the time, Marse Jesus come upon a crowd of peoples all just a shoutin' and a screamin' like they was fit to be tied."

"What were they screaming about?" Charlotte said, a spoon poised in her hand. Asking questions was half the fun of the story.

"That there was what Marse Jesus Hisself was wantin' to know," Daddy Elias said. "He push and shove His way right into the middle of that crowd, and what you think He see?"

"A wrestling match," Jefferson said.

"No, weren't no rasslin' match."

"A big snake," Charlotte said.

Daddy Elias shook his head and looked at Polly. She gave a wooden spoon a flustered wave. "I don't know, a dead body?"

"You almost right, Miz Polly! Marse Jesus, He seen them peoples holding big ol' rocks in they hands, and they's fixin' to throw them rocks right at a purdy woman lyin' there on the ground."

"Why?" Austin said. "That's horrible!"

"Them peoples, they think whatever crime that woman done is what be horrible. They thinkin' they was 'bout to punish her the way she deserve."

"Well, good heavens," Polly said. She pushed a sweaty strand of hair away from her face with the back of her hand. "Did she kill somebody?"

"It don't make no never mind to Marse Jesus what she done," Daddy Elias said. "He just bust through them people and throw Hisself in front of that there woman and say, 'Stop!' And them peoples say, 'No, she got to be punished for what she done wrong!'"

Polly stopped stirring the pot over the fire and twisted her mouth. "Isn't that true, though? Shouldn't people be punished for bad things?"

"Marse Jesus, He don't see it like that, not with them peoples. He look them all in they eyes, and He say, 'Onliest person here that ain't never done nothin' wrong can throw a stone at her.'"

Austin sat up straight. "But everybody's done *something* wrong!"

"'Zactly," Daddy Elias said, and then he just kept rocking.

"Supper's ready!" Polly said. "We even warmed your leftover cornbread."

Daddy Elias oohed over the chipped plate she put in front of him, while Austin's mind trailed off.

I know why he told that story, he thought. *He can't just say right out that Uncle Drayton was wrong. But what Jesus said just proves it—if Uncle Drayton has done some things wrong, he's got no business punishing Henry-James!*

Austin smiled smugly. It was nice to have Jesus on your side. At least then you knew you were always right.

It was nearly dark by the time the children returned to the Big House. Supper was over, and Aunt Olivia was in a worse stew than the chicken.

"I had to eat by myself!" she whined when she met them in the wide back hall. Scurrying behind her was her personal slave woman, Mousie, whose body matched her name. Austin watched in fascination, as always, as Aunt Olivia's double chins quivered.

"Your father is locked in his library, brooding," she said, "and Kady refused to come down after Mr. McCloud left—" She broke off then and gave a satisfied smile. "Of course, when you're love-sick, you don't want to eat."

"I don't think that's it at all," Austin said.

"And what would you know about it?" Aunt Olivia said, pulling in her chins so that they looked like three.

"I don't think she's lovesick either," Polly said. "And Garrison certainly doesn't act like he's in love with her."

Aunt Olivia put her plump, jeweled hands up to her ears. "I will not listen to this nonsense from you children any longer! Go up to Sally's room. She's eating there, and Josephine can bring your suppers up."

That was actually the children's favorite place to gather anyway, and Sally Hutchinson greeted them with a big Ravenal smile from where she sat on her couch. Her face was pale from being up and about all day, but her golden eyes were bright as she waved them all to chairs. Ria vacated hers to bring more.

"What's for supper?" Austin said. "I'm starving."

"You're an 11-year-old boy," Mother said. "Of course you're starving."

"Whatever it is, it can't be as good as what I just cooked at Daddy Elias's," Polly said.

Charlotte coughed, and Polly added, "Charlotte and I together."

Austin thought he heard Ria sniff. She was always either sniffing her disapproval or singing under her breath. She launched now into a soft tune that reminded him of the birds settling in for the night outside the window.

"I'm afraid there isn't much left of my supper," Mother was saying. "You'll have to wait for Josephine to bring up more."

Austin's eyes bugged at his mother's empty plate. "Did you eat all that?"

"I did," she said. "I am feeling so well, thanks to Ria."

"What are you doing for her, Ria?" Polly said. "I want to know all about taking care of the people on my plantation. Some men think a wife should be able to nurse her own household."

Charlotte rolled her eyes at Austin as Ria politely explained Mother's diet and exercise regimen for Polly. Jefferson climbed into his mother's lap.

"Are you feeling so well that you can come out and teach me to roll a hoop?" he said.

"I am feeling so well, my love, that I am thinking you and Austin and I should go back and join your father soon."

Austin felt his mouth drop open.

"It's just a thought now," she said quickly. "Don't start packing your trunk!"

Austin wasn't sure he wanted to pack his trunk. He wandered to the table beside his mother's bed and looked into the serious face of his father, Wesley Hutchinson, which stared solemnly out at him from the brass-framed picture.

I want to see you, Father, he wanted to say to it. *I have so much to tell you, and you would always listen—not like some people.* But he gave a weighty sigh as he went to the window and looked down on Canaan Grove as it tucked itself into the autumn night. *What about all of this, though?* he thought. *I've never been as happy anywhere as I've been here. I never even had friends before I came here.*

He felt as if he were being torn in half. He pulled in his shoulders and leaned into the glass.

As he blinked at his reflection, his eye was caught by movement below. Someone was running across the lawn, away from the Big House, with a cape trailing out behind like a wing. Austin watched curiously, and as he did, the figure turned to look back up at the house—as if she didn't want anyone to see her leaving.

Austin drew in his breath.

It was Kady . . . and it looked like she was running away.

osephine arrived with a tray full of smoked oysters and rice and Austin's favorite Brown Betty dessert. But he slid past her in the doorway, rocking her wide figure sideways.

"Austin?" his mother said. "Aren't you eating?"

"Later," he called back to her.

He tore toward the back stairs and skidded across the wide hall.

"Why do I hear running in this house?" he heard Aunt Olivia say as he slammed the door behind him. He didn't have to hear her to know she added, "And don't slam that door! Drayton, those Yankee children have absolutely no manners!"

Austin paused on the top step and squinted off in the direction where he'd seen Kady running. It had looked like she'd been headed into the maze of formal gardens Uncle Drayton had his slaves tend. Austin could just see the trailing edge of her deep purple cape as it disappeared behind a wall of camellias. Craning his neck to keep the cape in sight, Austin charged off after her. He was huffing like a steam engine when he found her in a heap under a magnolia tree.

"Whew!" he said. "I'm glad you stopped. I thought you were

running away." He dropped down beside her at the edge of the well-raked sand path. Only then did he realize Kady was crying. Her shoulders were jerking, and her sobs were like punches. These were angry tears.

"I never saw you cry before," Austin said. "You must be fit to be tied about something."

She looked up at him, face swollen and blotchy and miserable, hands clutching the notebook in which Austin knew she wrote poetry. "Good choice of words, Austin," she said. "I might as well be tied. I have about as much freedom as one of our darkies!"

Austin felt his eyes widen. "You mean they really are going to make you marry that Garrison McCloud person?"

Kady gave him a grim look. "Not him—yet. But somebody."

"You don't want to get married?" Austin said. "I don't blame you. I don't see the sense in it, you know?"

"I have absolutely no control over my life!" Kady said fiercely—as if Austin hadn't said a word. "There is so much I want to do, so much I want to change about this wretched world. And after all I've learned from Aunt Sally since she came here, I know I can do it. I know I can make things different." She doubled up both fists. "And all Mama and Daddy can think about is finding me a husband!"

Austin hugged his knees and warmed up to the conversation. "So, what kinds of things can you make different? You mean like teaching the slaves?"

"That's just a start," she said. She rubbed impatiently at the tears left on her cheeks. "That's all I can do right now. But there's so much more."

"Like what?"

"Once I get them educated, I'd like to see every one of them go free—and not just ours, but every slave in the South. And I'd like to see them treated like equals to people like my father."

Austin stared at her. "Does Uncle Drayton know you think that way?"

She gave him a dull smile. "You see that I still have all my teeth. Of course he doesn't know. He'd do worse than marry me off if he did."

Austin felt his chest puffing out. "I always knew you were an abolitionist like us!" He scrambled up onto his knees. "Hey, Mother is talking about going back north. You should come with us! Leaving wouldn't be so bad with you along!"

He was already spinning out a scenario of smuggling Charlotte and Henry-James along, too, when Kady shook her dark-haired head at him.

"Think about it, Austin," she said. "They have plenty of abolitionists in the North. They even have Sojourner Truth traveling all over speaking to people. You know, the black woman?"

Austin knew all about Sojourner Truth. She was a former slave who could get even hostile crowds of spitting white men to listen to her tell firsthand stories about the horrors of slavery.

Kady shook her head again, until her hair came loose from its chignon at the base of her neck. "I'm needed here," she said. "This is where my work's going to be."

"But how are you going to do that? Uncle Drayton already locked you in your room once for days."

"I don't know yet, but I'm sure not going to be able to do it married to a hotheaded little soldier like Garrison McCloud! All he could talk about today was standing behind a cannon and defending the noble cause of the South by blowing the heads off a bunch of plug-ugly Yankee mudsills—" She stopped short and rolled her eyes. "I'm sorry, Austin. I shoot off my *mouth* like a cannon."

Austin shrugged good-naturedly. "That's all right. I do the same thing. Charlotte told me today she thinks my mouth is going to get me in big trouble someday."

Kady grunted. "Maybe we'll share a cell."

Austin laughed, but Kady cut it off with a sudden finger to her lips. Austin listened, too—and heard a tiny voice, peeping from amid the sleepy crickets.

"Miz Kady?" it said. "You out here, Miz Kady?"

Kady winced. "That's Mousie," she whispered. "I bet Mama sent her out looking for me." She gazed longingly at the note-book on her lap. "I wanted to do some writing. I have to write about all this before I go to sleep or I'm going to explode! If I go in, Mama will have me in her room fussing over my hair and telling me how to win Mr. McCloud's little ol' heart."

Austin stood up. "Don't worry," he whispered. "I'll hold her off. You run!"

Kady nodded gratefully and, clutching her journal to her, darted off beyond the magnolia. Austin took only a second to note that its Latin name was *Magnolia grandiflora* before he rushed to meet Mousie.

When she saw him, the tiny flea of a woman jumped and let out a squeal so high-pitched that he could barely hear it. Austin put his hand to his chest.

"I'm sorry, Miss Mousie!" he said. He tried to get Uncle Drayton's southern gentleman lilt in his voice. "Did I startle you?"

She didn't seem to know whether to shake her head or nod. She looked anxiously past him.

"It's getting dark out here," Austin said. "And spooky. Don't you think this Spanish moss looks like witches's fingers pointing down at us? But don't worry, Miss Mousie, there's nothing to be afraid of. In the first place, did you know that it is not Spanish— they don't even have it in Spain. I've read that, though I've never been there myself. I hope to go someday, though. I've always wanted to see a bullfight." He sucked in a giant breath and kept on. "Anyway, not only that, but it isn't even moss. It's a fungus.

I haven't got the Latin name for that yet—I'm going to have to look it up. But I do know a lot of others. I like the way they feel in my mouth when I say them. Listen to this—*Osmanthus fragrans*. That's the sweet olive. *Camellia japonica*—camellia, of course."

Mousie stood with her little O of a mouth stiffened like a zero as Austin spun out a list of genus and species.

"*Daphne odora*," he said finally. "I don't know what that stands for yet, but I think it would make a good name for a girl— if a person were to want to have children, which I, of course, don't. I've had enough of them with my little brother."

Mousie blinked and swallowed, and Austin stole a glance beyond the magnolia tree. Kady must be long gone by now.

"Well, like I said, Miss Mousie," Austin said, "it's getting too dark for you to be out here by yourself, what with the *catulus felinus* out and all. May I escort you back to the Big House?"

He put out his elbow the way he'd seen Garrison McCloud do, and Mousie slipped her hand timidly inside his elbow and tripped along beside him.

"Miss Mousie?" he said. "You never did tell me why you were out here wandering around by yourself."

She didn't have to answer. A shrill voice scraped the night like a rusty nail running down a pail.

"Mousie!" it cried from the back porch. "Where you be? Missus want to know did you find Miz Kady yet?"

Austin smothered a grin. Yeah, it sure was nice to know what Jesus wanted you to do.

Cornhusking day dawned bright and November-crisp. The leaves, Daddy Elias said, "was at they purdiest—like the Lord been up all night a-paintin' on them." Austin treated everyone to an explanation of why the leaves turned colors in the autumn while they helped set up long tables outside for the feast and watched the slaves pile up bushel after bushel of corn for "peelin'."

"I don't know what you talkin' 'bout," Henry-James said when Austin was through.

"Never mind," Austin said. "Are you ready for the wrestling match?"

As if he were following a cue in a play, a dark-haired, big-headed figure stepped up. "I know I'm ready—readier'n I ever been!"

Austin snorted at the white boy. "Seems like you would have learned your lesson the other day. Henry-James whupped the tar out of you!"

Henry-James himself cut his eyes away, but the white boy looked green-eyed right at him and jerked his big head back to get rid of the stubborn sliver of hair. It fell right back over his too-high forehead.

"He didn't whup me no such thing," the boy said. His mouth barely moved from its tight line. "I'd a won if I hadn't gotten pulled off him."

"*You* got pulled off?" Austin said. "Seems to me my Uncle Drayton saved your hide by pulling *him* off *you!*"

The boy lurched toward Austin. A voice from a few yards away stopped him.

"Narvel!" a man growled. "Get over here and help me!"

Narvel didn't take his eyes off Austin as he backed away a few steps. "I'm comin', Daddy," he said through the slit-mouth. Then he squeezed his green eyes at Austin. "You seen the last of Narvel Guthrie even lookin' like he's bein' whupped. You just wait."

Austin puffed out his chest as Narvel turned and strutted, lopey-legged, toward his father. But Charlotte poked him soundly in the ribs.

"You know what, Austin?" she said. "Sometimes you just don't know when to hush up."

"What was that all about?" Polly floated up to them, wearing a puffy-sleeved jacket, which she tugged daintily.

Charlotte didn't say anything.

Austin grinned triumphantly at Henry-James. "Henry-James has got his wrestling partner running scared," he said.

"No, Massa Austin," Henry-James said, scowling until his eyebrows hooded his black eyes. "I think you just made him madder'n a soakin' wet hen."

"Don't worry!" Austin said. "We're the winners. Don't you ever listen to Daddy Elias when he tells those stories?"

Polly lost interest in answering. She took a quick little breath and nervously patted her curls—which, Austin noticed, actually looked like curls today instead of pieces of hay.

"How did you get them to do that?" Austin said.

But Polly strolled off in the direction of a broad-shouldered blond boy who stood on the back porch exhibiting his Citadel uniform.

"Good grief," Charlotte said. "Why in the world would you wear a uniform to a cornhusking?"

"To impress the pantaloon lace off Kady," Sally Hutchinson said. She stopped beside them, her arm linked through Ria's and her face beaming from beneath the brim of a straw hat. "I don't know about Kady, but it's certainly working on Polly."

They watched as Polly positioned herself at the foot of the porch steps and appeared to be engrossed in carrying baskets of apple pies and trays of smoked oysters to the picnic tables.

"Be sure you don't drop those now, Josephine," they heard her say. "Our people don't want dirty food."

And then she glanced demurely over her shoulder at Garrison McCloud.

"Look at that!" Charlotte said. "She's practically throwing

herself at him! Why doesn't she just hold up a sign that says, 'Pick me'?"

"Poor thing," Ria murmured under her breath. "She done set her cap for him, and that's downright hopeless."

But just then Kady appeared at the back door, a few steps from Garrison. He flashed her a smile and, to Austin's amazement, sent one just as brilliant down at Polly.

"Well, would you look at that," Sally Hutchinson said.

Maybe he thinks Polly looks different now, too, Austin thought. And then he was tired of watching people court. It was definitely one of the few things he *didn't* want to know about.

"When is it going to start?" he said.

"Look like right 'bout now," Henry-James said.

He pointed to the stack of corn, piled higher than Austin's head. Uncle Drayton didn't raise corn to sell, the way he did rice. The best of this huge crop would be used for the family's food. The rest would fatten the hogs and cows, and the shucks would go for stuffing the slaves' mattresses and scrubbing the wide plank floors in the Big House to a polish with lye.

Muscle-armed Isaac, the biggest, strongest slave at Canaan Grove, climbed on top of the pile. The rest of the slaves hurried over and gathered around him, until there was a sea of floppy-brimmed hats and many-colored head scarves. The black faces were shiny and expectant.

There were hundreds of them—field workers and boatmen, carpenters and cooks, coopers and tanners, weavers and stock minders. A rhythm of patting and clapping started as the black-smiths, bricklayers, and seamstresses joined them, along with the butchers, barbers, gardeners, and maids, and the pantry minders, tinsmiths, and baby keepers.

Austin watched them happily for a few minutes and even tried to clap along with them, although he wasn't very good at it. But as something occurred to him, he stopped and felt his puffed-up chest cave in.

After today's feast, not one of them who spent the afternoon shucking the corn would get another bite of it. Even the poor whites who stood around the edges watching would be allowed to take some home as part of their payment. But the slaves tasted corn only once a year.

Just then a different kind of clapping burst out, and a cheer arose that Charlotte, Sally, and Jefferson joined in on. Even Bogie began to bay as Daddy Elias came forward and a wooden crate was produced for him to stand on. Henry-James was there to help him onto it, and the old man held up a crusty hand to the swarm. There was at once a respectful silence.

"Now, you chilrun knows it been my job since I was nothin' but a young'un to lead the singin' at the cornhuskin'," Daddy Elias said to them.

There were hoots from the young bucks, but Daddy Elias shushed them with a hand and a smile from his spoon-shaped mouth. "The good Lord blessed me them years, but He done carried that gif' on to somebody else now." He bowed his snowy head at Henry-James. "And he gonna raise his voice to the Lord."

There were wild shouts of "Amen" and "Thank you, Jesus." Henry-James was lifted up to the top of the pile with Isaac like a hero onto shoulders. Austin felt his chest swelling up again.

If he has to be a slave, at least he's an important one, Austin thought.

"Brothers and sisters!" Henry-James sang out in his rich, almost-man voice. "We gon' husk some corn!"

It was a glorious thing to watch—Henry-James throwing his head back to lead the singing, Isaac tossing corn down to his fellow workers, and the slaves tapping their feet and reaching their hands up and squeezing their faces in song.

"Don't we get to shuck, too, Austin?" Jefferson shouted above the noise. "Those other white people are. I wanna do it!"

"Of course you can," Sally Hutchinson said. She already had her gray-striped sleeves rolled up and was headed into the crowd. "I wouldn't miss this for anything."

It seemed nobody wanted to miss it. Even Aunt Olivia sat her plump, dainty self in a big straw-woven chair with a cushion on it and pulled off corn husks, her rings sparkling in the sun. Of course, Mousie stood beside her, dabbing her mistress's forehead with a lace hanky between every ear of corn.

Austin sat on the ground with Charlotte and Jefferson, grabbing husk after husk and ripping it down and revealing silky hair and shiny rows of kernels like uneven teeth.

I bet Polly wishes her teeth were even this color, Austin thought. But this time he didn't say it. *Charlotte would be proud of me. I* do *know when to keep my mouth shut*.

The singing, husking, and merriment went on until the entire huge stack was gone.

"Now remember!" Aunt Olivia cried out to them all at one point. "The first unmarried person to find a red ear will be the next to be married."

She flashed a dimpled grin at Kady, who was sitting on a bench next to Garrison McCloud. Austin snickered. Garrison was trying to help Kady pull off a husk. She snatched it away from him and tore it off herself in one sure rip.

Charlotte peeked cautiously into a crack in the husk on the ear she was holding. "If I get a red one," she whispered to Austin, "I'm throwing it away."

"No," Austin said. "Give it to Polly!"

Charlotte grinned. "She'd never say another bad thing to me, would she?"

"I just hope Narvel Guthrie doesn't get it. Who would want to marry him?"

Austin looked around for Narvel and found him easily—sitting with a handful of other hired workers. Even they were smiling smiles that looked like grimaces and talking among themselves. Austin wanted to catch Narvel's eye to give him a smug look, but Narvel was too intent on his corn.

The only person who didn't seem to be enjoying herself was Ria. She picked up each ear with a solemn face and held her mouth tight as she took off its husk.

"I guess Ria doesn't want to get the red ear either," Austin said in a low voice.

"I don't think that's it," Sally Hutchinson said. Her own face went grim. "Cornhusking isn't Ria's favorite celebration."

"Why not?" Austin said.

"My father gave her a whipping when she was a young woman for cutting down a good cornstalk."

"That wasn't very fair!" Austin said. "I'm sure she didn't do it on purpose!"

Mother's golden-brown eyes took on a gleam. "Well, *I'm* not so sure about that. Ria hated my father. Sometimes she did things, just small things, to his property to get back at him."

That set off little sparks of interest in Austin's head. But before he could ask even the first of a whole line of questions, there was a squeal from the direction of the bench.

"Oh, my!" Polly cried. "Garrison's got the red ear!"

Amid the calls and clapping, Garrison held up a brick-colored ear of corn and sparkled one of his smiles at the crowd.

"My, my!" Aunt Olivia chirped from her chair. "Now, I wonder what that means!"

"It means he's going to marry Kady, doesn't it?" Jefferson said—loudly.

Polly glared at him. So did Kady. Garrison just kept smiling, and Uncle Drayton strode over and clapped him on the back.

"All Mama and Daddy can think about is finding me a husband,"

Kady had said to Austin. But a stupid red ear of corn couldn't mean anything, except that something had gone wrong with a seed. It was called a mutation. He'd read about that.

Still, he watched as Garrison held out both of his arms, one to Kady and one to Polly, and led them to the tables, where food was piled nearly as high as the corncobs had been.

Austin was getting pretty used to delicious food in enormous amounts. He and the Ravenals ate like this almost every day. What was more delicious to him was watching the slaves load up their plates and gather in suddenly quiet groups under the trees to devour the banquet with mussel shell spoons or their fingers. Most of the little ones skipped the ham and the chicken pie and the sweet potatoes and went right for the apple pies and the Brown Betty and the sugar-topped pan dowdy. Austin didn't blame them. Charlotte had told him they wouldn't get to eat like this again until Christmas.

Henry-James couldn't eat with Lottie and Austin. He had to wait on Uncle Drayton and, as it turned out, Garrison McCloud, too. Henry-James's black face was smooth as he filled Garrison's plate for him and brought him napkins, drinks, and second helpings. But Austin knew he wasn't thinking welcome thoughts about the cocky young soldier.

Austin, on the other hand, was thinking about the wrestling match. As the sun started heading for the tops of the tallest pines and oaks to the west and the dishes were all cleared away, Uncle Drayton stood up and brushed his hands together.

"I think we have some business to tend to!" he said.

The slaves responded with delighted whooping, and they immediately gathered into little knots around the strapping men of the plantation. Austin looked around for Narvel Guthrie. He couldn't see him, but he guessed he was in the midst of a dusty-looking cluster of white people. Narvel's father was among them, pointing his finger but never moving his mouth.

Austin grinned and crossed his arms over his chest. "This is going to be wonderful, Lottie," he said. "You just wait and see if it isn't."

Chapter Four

The first few matches were amazing to watch, which Austin did with Bogie beside him so he could duck his face behind the dog's big head whenever it looked as if someone was going to be squeezed down to the size of a snake. But after every tangle of sweat-shiny black bodies, the two men would stand up and hug each other, teeth gleaming, no matter which one Uncle Drayton declared the winner.

Isaac, of course, won for his group, but the slaves all cheered just as frantically for the others. By the time Isaac's arm was raised in victory, Austin was hoarse himself.

"When is it going to be Henry-James's turn?" Jefferson asked. "I want to see him whup the tar out of that ol' boy with the head like a watermelon."

"Jefferson!" Mother cried. "Now that was ugly!"

"Junior match now!" Uncle Drayton shouted. "For Canaan Grove, Ravenal's Henry-James!"

Austin shrieked and whistled as Henry-James stepped forward, stripped down to his diaperlike drawers, his black skin covered in gooseflesh in the afternoon chill.

"I understand we have a wrestler from our hired help," Uncle Drayton said.

The slaves were silent as Narvel came forward. He was bare-chested and wore a saggy-bottomed pair of jeans pants. Austin was sure he'd never seen a skinnier boy. He was a twig next to stocky Henry-James.

Austin patted Bogie with satisfaction. "He's won before he even starts," Austin whispered under a floppy ear. Bogie licked his chops.

"Drayton?" Aunt Olivia said. "Why is your body slave fighting a white boy?"

"We don't have any other boys Henry-James's age and size," Uncle Drayton said.

"Are you sure this is right?"

She looked more like she wanted to say it most certainly was not. But Uncle Drayton laughed.

"It's all in fun, Livvy," he said. "It's not as if our darky were attacking his social better without my permission."

"Better?" Austin said under his breath. "Henry-James is better than him any day—every way you look at it."

Bogie whined, and Austin wrapped his arms around his neck.

"Don't worry, boy," he whispered to him. "We'll just see who's better, won't we?"

Uncle Drayton put one hand on the back of each boy's neck. "Shake hands," he said.

"Drayton, really!" Aunt Olivia cried.

He teased a grin at her. "I know. I was only funnin' you." He turned again to the boys. "You know the rules. First one pinned down to a count of five is the loser. No biting, no scratching, no hitting. This is a clean fight."

"Henry-James doesn't need to do any of that stuff," Austin whispered to Charlotte. "He can win fair and square."

"All right, boys," Uncle Drayton said. "Let the match begin!"

The words no sooner left his lips than Narvel put his head

down and dove straight into Henry-James's chest. Bogie gave a yelp and sprang back on his haunches. Austin pulled him back by the baggy skin on his neck.

"It's all right, Bogie," Austin said. "Henry-James isn't even going to get a scratch."

It seemed as if he were right. Almost calmly, Henry-James wrapped his arms around Narvel's shoulders so he couldn't move. Then letting go with one hand, he reached down and grabbed the white boy's leg. Caught off balance, Narvel buckled, and Henry-James twirled him around and pushed him straight to the ground, facedown. Henry-James was on top of him in a flash.

"Start counting, Uncle Drayton!" Austin cried.

"One!" Uncle Drayton shouted. "Two!"

But before he got to "Three," Narvel gave a yell and rolled himself over twice until he was free. He got to his knees, just in time for Henry-James to shove him gently with the heels of his hands and push him back down to the ground. With his hands on Narvel's shoulders and his knees firmly planted in his thighs, Henry-James looked down in the white boy's face.

"One!" Uncle Drayton called out. "Two! Three!"

Austin was wringing out Bogie's neck skin with both hands. Beside him, Charlotte peeked out from between her fingers. "Is he winning?"

"Yes!" Austin shrieked.

But just as the "Four" came out, Narvel suddenly arched his back and for an instant wobbled Henry-James to the side. In that same instant, he wriggled away, scrambled to his knees, and hooked his arm around Henry-James's head from behind. He held on to his own wrist with his other hand and looked victoriously at the tiny crowd of whites. They were going wild.

"Start countin', Ravenal!" Narvel's father shouted. "He's got him!"

"No!" Austin shouted. "That's a headlock! He doesn't have him pinned to the ground."

"What's a headlock?" Charlotte asked frantically. "How can he get out of that?"

Austin wasn't sure he could. Henry-James came up on his heels and struggled, but Narvel had a grip he wasn't turning loose. Austin had read about headlocks. The only way to get yourself free was to—

Do exactly what Henry-James did then. Letting go of Narvel's forearms where he'd been tugging, he reached behind him and with a mighty jerk knocked Narvel's elbow. Then he slithered loose as if he were coming out of a window. A surprised Narvel was once more knocked to the ground on his back. This time Henry-James flattened himself into the white boy until they looked like one person—and Narvel didn't move.

"He's won, he's won!" Austin shouted, almost loud enough to drown out Uncle Drayton's painfully slow counting.

"One . . . two . . . three . . ."

Charlotte grabbed on to Austin's arm with both hands and hugged it. Austin jumped up and down, joggling her with him.

"Four, fi—"

But suddenly there was a scream—so agonized that it brought everybody to a stop in mid-cheer. Henry-James came up off Narvel, doubled over and heaving as if he were about to throw up his part of the feast.

And then he did, right there on the ground. Ria ran to him and curved herself over him like a shell. Henry-James's choking made Austin himself want to vomit.

Charlotte plastered her hand over her mouth, and Kady left Garrison to fly to Henry-James's other side. Polly put her face into Garrison's shoulder, and he patted her hand.

"Mousie!" Aunt Olivia cried. "I need my hanky!"

"What in blue blazes!" Uncle Drayton cried. "What's wrong with you, boy?"

The only reply was more retching.

"Answer me!" Uncle Drayton said.

"For pity's sake, Daddy!" Kady said. "Can't you see he's sick?"

By now, Narvel had pulled himself up off the ground and was standing looking down at Henry-James. His rib cage was pulsing in and out as if he couldn't get his breath. Most of his stringy black hair was hanging down into his eyes.

"I guess this means I won," he said.

"I'd say so," said his father behind him.

There was a smattering of applause from the poor whites.

"No!" Austin cried. "He didn't win! You have to pin your opponent down to a count of five. Narvel didn't do that!"

"The darky quit!" Narvel spat out through his slot-for-a-mouth.

"I bet you did something to him. He wouldn't just vomit like that! I bet he did something, Uncle Drayton!"

"I didn't do nothin' to make him vomit!" Narvel shot back.

"I cannot listen to such talk!" Aunt Olivia said with an elaborate whimper. "Mousie, help me to the house. Where is that nurse? I think I'm going to faint!"

"Mama, you're fine!" Kady said. "Henry-James needs her now."

Aunt Olivia recovered from her swoon long enough to spear a look at Kady before she wobbled off, with Mousie beside her, tottering under her mistress's weight.

Uncle Drayton looked from Austin to Narvel to Henry-James, his eyes growing narrower with every glance. "Can you talk, boy?" he said to Henry-James.

"Yes, Marse Drayton," he answered in a quavering voice.

"Bless his heart," Sally Hutchinson said. "Drayton, the boy is ill. Can't you leave him alone?"

"I'm sure he's well enough to defend the honor of his home," Drayton said.

"So much for 'all in fun,' " she said bitterly. She gathered her skirts up around her and marched off toward the Big House, dragging a protesting Jefferson with her. Austin didn't move.

"Sit up now, boy," Uncle Drayton said. "Look me in the eye and tell me what made you put on such a spectacle in front of your missus."

"Tell him, Henry-James!" Austin shouted as Kady helped the slave boy lift his head from the ground. His eyes, however, stayed firmly rooted to it.

"I got him pinned down, Marse Drayton," he said. "I hear you sayin' 'Five', and then he get his knee up and pump me with it."

"You see that!" Austin shouted.

Narvel doubled his fists and waved them. "I didn't do nothin' like that!"

Uncle Drayton poked Henry-James lightly with his toe. "Look at me."

Slowly, Henry-James tilted his face upward. His chin was dripping, and his eyes were ashamed. Austin wanted to hit someone.

"Are you telling me the truth, boy?" Uncle Drayton said. "You know I rarely whip a slave, unless I catch him in a lie. If you are lying to me, I will have you over that barrel, and fast. Answer me. Are you tellin' the truth?"

"Yes, Marse Drayton," Henry-James said. "I's tellin' you the honest truth."

"He's a lousy cuffee liar!" Narvel cried. "How could I get him with my knee? He had me pinned down!"

"He had you pinned down when I said 'Five'?" Uncle Drayton said.

"Yeah!"

"I seen it myself!" said Narvel's father in his growling voice.

Uncle Drayton narrowed his eyes at the older Guthrie this time. "Well, then, Micah," he said, "if I take your son's word for it, it looks like my boy won."

Narvel bolted forward and threw himself at Henry-James, knocking Ria one way and Kady the other. Before Austin could even move, Narvel was straddling Henry-James and pummeling his chest with his fists.

"Get him off, Guthrie!" Uncle Drayton shouted. "Get him off or so help me I'll do it myself!"

Micah Guthrie didn't move so much as an eyelid. Kady hauled herself up and crawled toward Narvel. But she couldn't get there before Bogie.

With a snarling leap, the big dog crashed into Narvel's arm, knocking him sideways and scrambling on top of him on all fours. He bared his teeth in the white boy's face, and he growled like a mother bear.

"Get him off!" Narvel screamed. "He's gonna bite my face off! Get him off!"

"Get that dog off before I kill him!" Micah Guthrie said.

Henry-James's head came up off the ground where he still lay. "Bogie!" he said sharply.

Bogie looked at him, his eyes pleading for just one bite.

"No," Henry-James said.

Still muttering under his breath, Bogie trotted over to Henry-James and licked the side of his face from chin to hairline.

"Now I'll thank you to leave my property, Guthrie," Uncle Drayton said. "And I'll thank you to do it right quick-like."

It didn't take a minute for Micah Guthrie and the other poor whites to gather up Narvel and hustle him off to their farm wagons in the stable yard, all grumbling like Bogie as they glowered back over their shoulders. Uncle Drayton watched them with the interest already fading from his face.

"I'm glad the harvest is done," he said. "I want nothing more to do with their kind." He dusted his hands together, as if to wipe away the Guthries as well as dirt. "The sun is nearly down," he said to what was left of the cornhusking crowd, "and I have yet to see a double shuffle from any of my slaves. Where is the music? What about the dancin'?"

Obediently, the slaves scattered to find their banjos, fiddles, and drums. But every one of them cast a lingering look down at Henry-James as they passed by, their eyes showing fear. Charlotte was already on her knees next to him when Austin joined them. Bogie whimpered and nudged Austin's elbow with his big head. Austin patted him absently and looked down at his friend.

"Are you hurt bad?" he asked.

"Best meal I had all year, Massa Austin," Henry-James said in a still-shaky voice. "And it's already gone."

"Is the boy all right?" Uncle Drayton said.

"Yes, Marse Drayton," Ria said automatically—although Henry-James still looked a little sickly as far as Austin was concerned.

"Good," Uncle Drayton said. "Then let's get this mess cleaned up."

Ria started to get up, but Kady caught her by the arm.

"I do it," Isaac said softly from behind them. He already had a bucket and a shovel.

Henry-James sat up, warily watching Uncle Drayton as he strode off toward the Big House. Even as they watched, he turned around and pointed his finger. "Good fight, boy," he said. "You did Canaan Grove proud."

Henry-James nodded a thank you. Uncle Drayton walked off with Garrison McCloud hurrying to catch up with him and Polly following after, trying to look as if she weren't following after. Austin nudged Henry-James gently on the arm.

"See?" he said. "I told you we were the winners."

Ria sniffed and got to her feet. "I gots to go see to Miz 'Livia," she said gruffly.

"I don't know what got into Narvel," Kady said when she was gone. "I know he acts like a scoundrel, but I never took him for a cheater."

"Do you know him?" Austin asked.

"We've talked some," Kady said. "We have a lot in common."

Austin gave a snort. "Not as much as you thought. He's a lying little sinner."

"Mmmm-mmmm, Lordy," said a voice behind them.

Austin looked up at Daddy Elias, who was there rubbing an old hand across his spoon-shaped mouth.

"You were right," Austin said to him. "Jesus doesn't like people to pretend to be all good and then cheat and lie."

"No," Daddy Elias said. "I don't reckon He does."

The music was firing up on the porch and several slaves appeared with torches, which they stuck in the ground. In the golden light, the black men and women began tapping their toes and kicking their heels, their bright skirts and scarves flashing like snippets of fire.

Henry-James got to his feet and tottered for only a second before he looked strong and sure again. Kady handed him his knee-long shirt to slip on over his head.

"Now I don't want any argument from you, Henry-James," she said. "As long as Daddy doesn't need you for the rest of the evening, I am going to keep an eye on you myself."

"Us, too," Austin said, nodding toward Charlotte.

Henry-James ducked his head and muttered something about

a whole lot of fuss, but Austin could tell by the way he showed the gap between his teeth that he was pleased. Charlotte took his arm on one side and Kady took the other. Austin walked backward in front of him.

"I have a question for you, Henry-James," he said.

"You do?" Kady said, grinning. "What a surprise."

"What did it feel like when you had that little sneak down on the ground?"

"Austin!" Charlotte wailed. "I don't want to hear about that."

Austin nodded. He could always ask Henry-James about that later.

The slaves danced under the big orange wafer of a moon until even the young ones were tired. As Josephine and the other kitchen maids passed around bowls of popcorn and boiled peanuts, the music slowed down into the almost magical sounds of "Swing Low, Sweet Chariot" and "Jacob's Ladder."

Austin stretched out on his back and closed his eyes to listen. *Everything's pretty good right now*, he thought. He liked the smug feeling in his chest. It was good knowing he wasn't a rotten egg like Narvel Guthrie.

His thoughts were interrupted by Kady's voice and Charlotte poking him in the side. Kady sounded like she was arguing with someone. Austin opened his eyes and propped himself up on his elbow.

"I am going to sit right here and look after Henry-James," Kady was saying.

"Now come on, Miss Kady," said Garrison McCloud. "Just a few minutes in the garden? It's important."

"I'm not allowed to walk with gentlemen alone at night," she said.

"Your father already gave me his permission."

Kady's eyes flashed, and Austin caught Charlotte's glance. She was smothering a giggle with her hand.

Kady's neck arched. "Oh, he did!" she said. "Without bothering to ask *me?*"

Garrison McCloud didn't look the least bit deflated. "I love your spunk, Miss Kady, but do you know that you are making a complete fool out of me in front of these children?" He glittered down a smile.

"Oh, no, not at all, Mr. McCloud," Polly said from a few feet away. "I don't think you are a fool or any such thing."

"But Miss Polly," Garrison said, "you aren't one of the children, now, are you?"

Austin thought he was going to be the one to throw up this time. Charlotte rolled her eyes into her head. Only Polly smiled—until Kady sighed and put up her hand.

"All right," she said. "I'll go, but for a few minutes, and that's all."

"You won't be sorry," they heard him say as he led her off toward the garden.

"Did you see that?" Polly said, her eyes fiery.

"See what?" Charlotte said.

"Kady barely gives him a second glance all day. But the very minute he and I are getting on so well, then she decides she's interested and sweeps him right out from under my nose!"

Austin had to admit that it had seemed that way. But for the second time that day he was getting tired of all this romantic intrigue.

"I don't want to hear another word about courting!" he said.

It was one wish that didn't come true.

He and Jefferson were already tucked into bed that night, and Austin was sleepily drifting in and out among his prayers and thoughts of wrestling matches and all the questions he was going to ask Henry-James the next day, when he was jolted awake by angry voices downstairs.

Leaving Jefferson sleeping, Austin tiptoed out of his room to the front stairs above Uncle Drayton's library. He grinned when he saw Charlotte, Polly, and Tot already sitting on the steps with their faces poked between the poles of the stair rail.

"Listen," Charlotte whispered when she saw him. Her eyes were in big, serious circles.

"Kady Sarah Ravenal!" Aunt Olivia was shrieking. "This is the worst thing you have ever done to us. The worst thing *ever!*"

Chapter Five

"**W**hat have I done to *you*, Mama?" Kady said. "This is *my* life we're talking about."

"What did she do?" Austin whispered to Charlotte.

"She gave Garrison McCloud the mitten," Polly hissed. She was looking pretty pleased about the whole thing.

"She gave him a mitten?" Austin whispered. "What for?"

"It means she jilted him, silly," Polly said. "He asked her to marry him and she said no."

"Of course she did. She doesn't even like him—"

But Polly shushed him with her hand. The volume of the voices below was climbing fast.

"I have been waiting since the day you were born to plan a wedding for you!" Aunt Olivia was saying tearfully.

"I'm supposed to marry a man I don't love just so you can have a party to impress everyone in Charleston?"

"No, I'm talking about your happiness! You're going to end up an old maid!"

"Mama, I'm 17 years old. I'd hardly call this my last chance!"

"I wouldn't be too sure of that, young lady," Uncle Drayton said.

Austin felt himself stiffening when he heard his uncle's voice. It didn't have its usual molasses-rich sound. It was steely cold and hard.

"Really, Daddy, am I that unlovely?" Kady said.

Austin saw Polly nod.

"That is not what I mean and you know it! You are well aware that we do not have the social position we once had."

"Drayton!" Aunt Olivia cried. "Please don't say that!"

"Olivia, get your head out of the sand. As long as I refuse to go along with these secessionist Fire Eaters, we are nothing more than outcasts in South Carolina. We're no better off in the eyes of society than the Guthries."

They could hear Aunt Olivia gasping all the way upstairs. Polly looked as if she were going to vault the banister.

"Garrison McCloud knows all of that, but he is still willing—anxious, even—to take you as his wife, Kady. You may never have another opportunity to marry a man of wealth and social standing."

"What if I don't want a man of wealth and social standing?" Kady snapped back. Austin could imagine her dark eyes on fire, her thick curls tossing everywhere. "What if I want a man who shares my beliefs and cares about the things I care about?"

"What could possibly be so different between you and Garrison McCloud?" Aunt Olivia said with goose-bump shrillness. "You have both been raised in South Carolina in the lap of luxury. You are young people of good upbringing and manners—"

"I couldn't care less about manners! Don't you see that?"

"You'd better start caring about them, and a lot of other things as well," Uncle Drayton said. "As a woman, you don't have any other choice. If you do not marry a man of means, what's to become of you?"

There was a dead pause. Polly cocked her head and leaned closer so she wouldn't miss a syllable.

"Then I'm no better off than one of your slaves, Father," Kady said finally. Her voice was low, as if she were about to threaten someone. "My choices have been made for me, and I'm to live my life the way you tell me to. Why don't you just throw me over a barrel and whip me?"

"Kady, don't be ridiculous!"

"No, do it! At least then it would be over with. I'd take a thousand whippings before I would ever marry Garrison McCloud or anyone like him. So break out the whip, Mr. Ravenal, and I'll meet you in the woodshed!"

"You will *not* speak to me that way!" Uncle Drayton cried.

Too late, Austin thought. *She just did.*

And he was glad. His heart pounded for Kady as the library door was flung open so hard that it slammed against the wall. The children scattered like chicks as Kady flew up the steps in a flurry of petticoats, nearly stepping on Austin's hand as he scrambled to get out of her furious way. He glanced down to see Uncle Drayton and Aunt Olivia in the hall looking up, cheeks reddening and eyes smoldering. The looks on their faces sent a spear through Austin.

At that moment, they looked as if they hated Kady. And he had never seen two people look more ugly.

The rustle of skirts stopped right behind him, and Austin twisted around to see Kady. Even in the dull gleam of the oil lamp in the socket on the wall, her face was coldly pale.

"Don't bother to lock me in my room this time," she said. "I can take care of that myself. I don't want to be a part of *this* household anyway."

She disappeared before her parents could get their mouths open.

By then, Austin's mother and Ria were standing outside their door. Mother ushered the four of them inside just as Uncle Drayton shouted, "This is not a show! Back to bed, all of you!"

I'll go to bed when I want to—not when you *tell me to!* Austin thought fiercely.

"Come on, all of you," his mother was saying. "Into the bed before you catch your death of cold."

It *was* November chilly in the bedroom, and they were all happy to pile into Sally Hutchinson's warm bed—one of their favorite places since last summer. Their best conversations seemed to happen there. Ria poked at the fire as Polly and Charlotte squeezed in on either side of Mother, and Tot and Austin both wrapped in quilts at the foot. Polly was the first to speak up.

"I'm *glad* Kady isn't going to marry him," she said with a decided nod. Tot, of course, nodded, too.

"Why?" said Charlotte. "So you can have him?"

"I'd marry him in a minute!"

"But you're only 14," Austin said.

Polly rolled her eyes and pushed her hair back up under the edges of her ruffled nightcap. "Well, you heard what Daddy said. It isn't going to be easy for us to find good husbands now that we're misfits. If someone should ask me—the right person, I mean—I think I should accept."

"Charlotte, too?" Austin said.

Charlotte kicked at him under the covers.

"Well, Polly," Sally Hutchinson said, "I'm glad Kady is refusing to marry him, too, but for a different reason."

Her voice was so sad that it got Austin's attention.

"There is nothing worse than being married to someone you don't love."

Polly stared at her. "I thought you loved Uncle Wesley!" she said.

"Oh, I do. I wasn't talking about myself."

She looked across the room, and Austin followed her gaze. She was watching Ria, whose lips were tight as she needlessly rearranged the fire.

Huh, Austin thought. *I never even wondered about her having a husband—or Henry-James having a father either.*

"What?" Austin said. "Are you talking about Ria?"

Mother nodded sadly. "I think now would be a good time to tell them your story, Ria. But only if you want to."

Although Ria looked as if she would rather do almost anything else, she sat on the edge of her chair by the bed and folded her hands stiffly in her lap. She looked over the tops of all their heads. "I weren't no older than Miz Kady when I set my heart on a black boy name of James. He live on another plantation, but he get a pass every chance he get to come see me. And sometime he even come without a pass."

"How romantic!" Polly said.

Charlotte and Austin exchanged disgusted glances.

"And so James, he ask Marse Ravenal if'n we could get married."

"Marse Ravenal was my father," Mother put in. "And Drayton's father, of course."

Austin wrinkled his nose. He'd heard enough about his grandfather to know he wouldn't have liked him at all.

"What did he say?" Polly asked.

"He say he don't believe in no slave o' his marryin' no slave from no other place. I belong to him, and he gonna decide who I'm gonna marry."

"That sounds familiar," Austin muttered.

"So what did you do?" Polly said. Her eyes were wide, and she was sitting straight up on the bed as if Ria were spinning a fairy tale. Austin wasn't sure it was all *that* interesting.

"I get to tell this part," Mother said. "I listened to Ria cry every night until I couldn't stand it anymore. And so, one night—it was June, wasn't it?"

Ria looked down at her lap and nodded.

"We met James in the woods, Ria and Daddy Elias and I, and

we took the broom, and we married them."

"The broom?" Austin said. "Don't you mean 'groom'?"

Mother smiled. "The tradition is that when a slave couple steps over a broomstick, they're declared married. Daddy Elias used all of God's words about marriage just like a preacher, and we prayed to the Lord to make it right. I know they were married in God's eyes."

"More married than I was two months later when Marse Ravenal tol' me I got to marry a boy here at Canaan Grove and missus give me a big weddin' celebration with a banquet and a cake they done baked in the Big House." Ria's eyes were bitter. "They wasn't no preacher—nobody didn't say nothin' 'bout the Lord. They just give us a party and tol' us we was married."

Polly folded her thin arms across her chest. "I just wouldn't have done it!"

Mother patted Polly's leg. "We'd all like to think we were that brave, but you know the slaves have absolutely no choice. They have to do what they're told."

"So go on with the story," Austin said. "What happened to James and that other guy?"

"Right after that," Ria said woodenly, "James, he got sold. I don't know where to. I ain't never see'd him again."

"Oh, no!" Polly cried.

"A year later, I married Wesley," Mother said. "I was determined to marry the man I wanted to—as much to honor Ria and James as for myself."

Ria nodded. "Right after Miz Sally married Wesley Hutchinson from Virginia and then tol' her daddy they was sellin' that there homestead and goin' north, Marse Ravenal he up and died." She looked at Polly. "You was a baby then, and that's when your daddy take over Canaan Grove. Henry-James, he was borned just a little while after that, and Miz 'Livia tol' me I got to name my boy after the old marse."

"That's right," Polly said. "Granddaddy Ravenal was named Henry—I remember that now." She shrugged. "I never even knew him."

"But you added the James," Charlotte said to Ria.

"I done that after that man I was s'posedly married to died of the fever just one week after Henry-James be borned."

Austin felt a pang. "So Henry-James has never really had a father."

"Not 'cept for Daddy 'Lias," Ria said. "And he done a real good job."

"He's done an excellent job," Mother said. "Henry-James is a fine young man, and I'm proud that he's my sons' friend."

They all sat in silence for a minute. Austin wasn't sure why, but it didn't seem right to speak. That wasn't a feeling he had often. When someone pounded on the door, they all jumped as if they'd been shot.

"Sally!" Uncle Drayton said from the hallway. "Is Kady in there with you?"

"Let him in, would you, Ria?" Mother said.

Uncle Drayton was the last person Austin wanted to see. He got off the bed and went stubbornly to the window with his back to the door. When it opened, he heard his uncle's crisp footsteps crossing to the bed.

"I see I have as much control over you two as I do over Kady," he said to Polly and Charlotte. "I told you all to go to bed."

"We're in bed, Daddy," Polly said.

Austin turned in surprise. That wasn't Polly's style. She usually did everything but pour honey on her father to stay on his good side. Austin was just in time to catch the angry glint in Uncle Drayton's eyes. Polly, Charlotte, and Tot scrambled from the bed and headed for the door. Austin turned back to the window in disgust.

"Don't look at me like that, Drayton," Mother said. "I'm not hiding Kady under the bed."

"You wouldn't tell me if you were," Uncle Drayton said.

"I have no need to hide Kady. I can tell you to your face how I feel about what's going on."

"And I'm sure you will, whether I want to hear it or not."

"I most certainly will. Do you remember, Drayton, that I never saw our father—never spoke to him again—after I married Wesley, because he was so incensed about my choice of a husband?"

"I'm not Henry Ravenal," Uncle Drayton said sharply.

"Really?" she said. "You could have fooled me."

"You cannot accuse me of being nearly the cruel man he was!"

"There are moments when I think you're right," Mother said. "I'm so proud of you for rebelling against the secessionists, for allowing your slaves to learn to read, for seeing the potential in Henry-James and working with him."

Austin had to agree with that. Still, there was a "but" in his mother's voice. He got perfectly still so he wouldn't be sent away before he heard what it was.

"But then there are times," she went on, "when you sound *exactly* like Henry Ravenal, and I just want to shake you and scream, 'Don't you hear yourself?' "

"I hear myself taking care of my daughters so they won't end up living miserable lives!"

"What do you know about their lives? When they grow up, those lives will belong to them, not you!"

"That's right," Austin murmured.

There was a sudden silence behind him.

"I know your views on child rearing are completely different from mine—just like your views on everything else," Uncle Drayton said. "But would you mind if we carried on this discussion without your son present?"

Austin turned around to protest, but his mother was already nodding toward the door. "Do you mind, my love?" she said. "Uncle Drayton and I need to talk alone."

He minded so much that he was about to explode, but he crossed reluctantly to the door. As he closed it behind him, he heard his mother say, "I'll tell you one thing, Drayton, I think *Austin* could manage this situation better than you're doing."

Austin smiled against the angry poking feeling in his back. *That's because I'm on the right side,* he thought. *And I bet Jesus is going to show me just what to do about this.*

Chapter Six

or the next several days, Kady came out of her room only to go out to the spring house to give the slave children their reading lessons. To Polly's disappointment, Garrison McCloud didn't come back to call, though Austin noticed that she was ready every day with her hair coiffed and her ruffles pressed. The only evidence that there had ever been a family fight was Aunt Olivia's constant sniveling into her hanky, which kept the handkerchief-toting Mousie busy. Even Uncle Drayton stayed holed up in his library.

Besides, there was something else happening that kept the children from thinking much about Kady's future at all. It was Henry-James's they were worried about.

Several days after the cornhusking, the slaves were gathered around the back porch to get their new clothes. Austin, Charlotte, and Jefferson sat on the railing, swinging their ankle jackboots and watching Henry-James being fitted into his first custom-made house servant's uniform. It had a coat of dark blue broadcloth and trousers of blue plush, and his vest was faced with red and trimmed in silver braid. It was as handsome as anything Uncle Drayton wore, Austin thought. But he wasn't thinking many kind thoughts about Uncle Drayton these days.

"What do the other slaves get?" Austin said. He nodded toward the line of black men that queued up in front of Aunt Olivia. Each one stepped forward as she called his name out of a book and gave her a deep bow before he walked away with his thin pile.

"The men get two of those cotton shirts and a pair of wool pants and a wool jacket," Charlotte said. "The women have to make their own clothes."

Austin saw Kady handing out the piles of blue-and-white and brown-and-white plaid cloth from big bolts for that, while Mousie counted out a needle, a skein of thread, and six buttons for each black woman.

Next to them stood Polly with the children lined up in front of her. As each one came forward, she rolled out some homespun from a bolt and held it up behind him. The bottom touched the floor, and she cut it off just above his head, once for a piece of white and once for a piece of red. Austin didn't have to ask what they'd be getting out of that. All he'd ever seen any of the black young'uns wear was a long shirt made out of sackcloth with no real pants underneath. He'd seen Ria sit by the fire in their cabin and stitch underwear for Henry-James out of sacks and bags. The thought of it made Austin itch.

"I'm glad my Tot gets more than this," Polly said as she measured out cloth for a woolly-headed little girl.

The house servants always looked almost elegant with their blue uniforms for the men and their starched aprons for the women. Austin knew that was because they were considered part of the house.

"I wouldn't have shabby draperies in my home," he'd heard Aunt Olivia say. "Why should I have ragged servants?"

"Why is Tot out here, then?" Austin said as he watched Polly's slave girl fidget in a fourth line on the lawn.

"It's shoe year," Polly said.

"What's that?"

"Every two years they get a pair of shoes," said Charlotte, "except for the children."

"I wish I was one of those children," Jefferson said. "I hate wearing shoes."

"You wouldn't if you *had* to go barefoot," Austin said. "Haven't you seen how cut-up Henry-James's feet get sometimes?"

He watched happily as Henry-James put his feet into a pair of ankle-high shoes on the porch steps below them. They had broad bottoms and big, flat heels, and Henry-James took his first few steps in them as if they were blocks of lead.

"See?" Jefferson said. "He hates them!"

"They don't fit yet," Charlotte said. "But they will after that." She pointed to two buckets, one of water and one of something greasy-looking. Austin wrinkled his freckled nose as Henry-James dipped his new boots once in the water and once in the grease.

"What is that?" he asked.

"Meat skin," Charlotte said. "Nasty, huh?"

Austin didn't get to answer. Uncle Drayton's voice trumpeted out as he opened the back door, and Austin felt his lip curling up when he saw who trailed out behind him onto the porch.

"What are the Guthries doing back?" Charlotte whispered to him.

Austin scowled and watched.

"All right, Micah," Uncle Drayton was saying. "You've talked me into it. But the moment your boy causes an instant of trouble, you are through here—for good!"

"Talked him into what?" Austin whispered.

"You're good workers, both of you," Uncle Drayton said as he wove Narvel and Micah through the lined-up slaves and out onto the grass. "I can use your help preparing the fields for the next planting. I'm expanding my production this year, but I don't want to buy any more slaves."

"They're gonna work here again!" Austin hissed.

"No!" Jefferson cried, out loud, of course. "I don't like them!"

Uncle Drayton's eyes lifted to the porch railing, and they settled not on Jefferson, but on Austin.

"The Guthries are in my employ," he said briskly. "I expect them to be left alone to do their work."

Don't worry, Austin thought bitterly. *I wouldn't go near that low-life boy.*

Narvel looked as if he felt that way and worse. He drilled his too-close-together green eyes into Austin, then darted them around until they found Henry-James.

"He'd better stay away," Charlotte whispered beside him. Austin looked down to see her hands balled into little fists. He would have laughed if he weren't thinking the same thing himself.

"*We'd* better look after Henry-James," he whispered back.

The next day, Uncle Drayton was brooding in his library all morning, and he sent Henry-James out to help repair the dikes that held the water in the rice fields during the growing season. Charlotte and Austin agreed to meet Henry-James at the well when he went for his water break. Jefferson tagged along, and he immediately tried to climb up on the well's stone wall.

"Don't, Jefferson!" Charlotte said. "You'll fall in and drown yourself!"

"How far down is it?" he said, still trying to get a foothold on a stone.

"Too far for anybody to get down there and fetch you out," Austin said. He leaned over to look down the well, and he couldn't help shivering. The water was darker than night and bottomless. None of them could swim, not even Henry-James. That well could swallow one of them up like a giant mouth before you could holler, "Help!"

"I could ride down in that," Jefferson said, pointing a chubby finger to the wooden bucket that swung on a rope over the well.

Austin eyed him critically. "*You* could, shrimp," he said. "You're light enough. See, it's a pulley system. I know how that works."

"You done read about it in a book."

Austin grinned up at Henry-James, and Jefferson ran to him as if he hadn't seen him in years.

"I don't care much 'bout how it work, Massa Austin," Henry-James said. "I just want to get me some water from it."

Although the autumn chill had settled in, the sun was bright and Henry-James's forehead was glistening with sweat.

"I'll do it," Charlotte said.

She jumped up and grabbed on to the crank and began to turn it. Slowly, the bucket creaked its way down on its rope and thunked into the water. It was harder to crank it back up, but Charlotte puffed and turned the handle.

The bucket sloshed up over the side of the well, and Charlotte dipped the ladle into it and handed it to Henry-James, who slurped it up gratefully.

"Don't be drinkin' it all, darky," said a voice behind them.

Austin didn't have to turn to know who it was. Nobody else but Narvel Guthrie always talked like he had his teeth gritted together. Austin stiffened and looked at the other three. Nobody was even glancing at Narvel, though Jefferson was sticking out his tongue furtively.

"Drink all you want, Henry-James," Austin said. "You've been working hard out there."

"Oh, and I ain't?" said Narvel.

It was hard, but Austin ignored him. Henry-James drank on, and Charlotte kicked at a pebble. Jefferson widened his mouth with both index fingers and waggled his tongue.

"You all treat that black boy like he's prince of the plantation!" Narvel said. "He ain't nothin' but a darky, y'know."

That Austin couldn't ignore. In spite of Charlotte's frenzied shaking of her head, Austin turned on Narvel.

"I'd be proud to say I was a darky," he said. "What I'd hate to have to say was that I was a lying, cheating, whining little white boy."

"Yeah!" Jefferson said.

Charlotte clapped her hand over his mouth. Henry-James kept on drinking.

"A lyin', cheatin', whinin' little white boy?" Narvel said. "You mean, like yourself?"

"No," Austin said. "I was talking about you—although you're not terribly smart, so I can see how you would have trouble understanding me."

"You think I ain't smart?" Narvel said. He spat out a laugh and left a string of a smile on his face. "Then you're the one who's stupid."

Austin could hardly keep from grinning from one earlobe to the other. This was going to be delicious. "Since we can't agree," he said, "I think we ought to have a contest."

"Contest?"

"Sure. We'll ask each other questions and whoever answers the most right is the smartest. Charlotte can keep score. I get to keep asking you until you get one right, and vice versa."

"I don't know nothin' 'bout no vicey-versey," Narvel said. His entire face looked like a question mark.

"That means 'the other way around,' " Jefferson said.

Austin smothered a smirk. "First question," he said. "What's the common name for *Quercus virginiana?*"

Narvel's line-mouth drooped into a triangle.

"Don't know?" Austin said.

"Uh-uh."

"Live oak," Austin said. "Let me give you an easier one. How about *Carya corpidormis?*"

"You ain't even speakin' English!" Narvel cried.

"Well, no, but it's simple Latin. You know that one, Henry-James?"

"That there carry-a-corpse would be a butternut hickory, Massa Austin," he said. His black eyes were riveted to the ground, but the gap between his teeth was showing happily.

"No more of them kind of questions," Narvel growled. "Pick somethin' else."

"All right," Austin said, shrugging casually. "What's the score, Charlotte?"

"Austin has two points, Narvel has none," she said.

"I know!" Narvel said. "I don't need no girl to tell me what the score is." He curled his lip at Henry-James. "Just like I don't need no girl gettin' my water out of the well for me."

Charlotte's golden-brown eyes turned to stone. Austin scrambled in his brain for another question.

"All right, Navel—"

"*Nar*-vel!"

"Right. Here's a really easy one. Anybody can get this one. Who is Sojourner Truth?"

"Who?"

"Abraham Lincoln?"

"Does he live around here?"

"Let me ask one!" Jefferson cried. He marched up to Narvel, hands on hips. "I bet you don't even know what gravididdy is!"

"I don't know!" Narvel cried. "And I don't care!"

With a sideways swat, he batted Jefferson away like a fly and charged straight ahead. Austin couldn't even snatch up the thought of running before Narvel drove his head into Austin's belly and hoisted him up over his shoulder. The ground spun before Austin's eyes as he was twirled, head and arms dangling over Narvel's back, feet locked against the white boy's chest like a pair of sticks in a vice.

"Put me down!" Austin shouted at him.

He pounded both fists against Narvel's backside, but he didn't twitch. His rear end might as well have been made of iron.

The boy turned faster, and Austin's breakfast threatened to come up his throat. He squeezed his eyes shut.

"Put me down!" he shouted again.

"Put you down? Sure, I'll put you down. Right down here!"

With a lurch, he stopped and began to let Austin's legs slip over his shoulders.

He's going to drop me on my head! Austin thought wildly. He pointed his arms down to brace himself and opened his eyes.

Below him was a solid wall of dank, black water.

Austin flailed his arms. They hit the damp side of the cold stone wall, and he screamed.

"What's the matter, smart boy?" Narvel's tight voice echoed in the well. "Can't you figure a way out? You know everything else!"

By now Austin could only feel Narvel's hands around his ankles. The rest of Austin dangled helplessly over the watery tunnel below.

"Don't drop me!" Austin screamed.

The iron-band fingers loosened, and Austin felt himself jerk. He yelled from the pit of his stomach and flung his hands out to catch at the wall. But the fingers tightened again, and Narvel's laughter bounced against the stone.

"Now who's the smart one?" he shouted down into the well. "Give me the right answer and I'll pull you out!"

"You're smart!" Austin cried. His head was throbbing with both fear and the blood that was rushing to it. He groped at the slippery stones on the wall. "Just don't let go of me!"

"Smarter than you?" Narvel called out.

"Yes! Please—"

"Smarter than your bratty little brother?"

"Yes!"

Austin would have said Narvel was wiser than Solomon him-self. Narvel's fingers were burning into his ankles, and the cave below was opened like a hollow mouth ready to swallow him.

Narvel howled. "Smarter than this *girl?* Smarter than this whinin' little colored boy who won't lift a finger to help you?" He gave a high-pitched hoot. "And he better not, 'cause if he touches me again, he's in *biiig* trouble!"

Austin went cold. He thought surely they had run for help by now. And Narvel was right. Uncle Drayton had said it himself: Henry-James couldn't attack his "social better" without permis-sion.

Uncle Drayton doesn't care if I die or not! he thought fran-tically. *And I am gonna die. I'm gonna die right here!*

"Lottie!" he shouted. "Henry-James! Run for help!"

But his words were lost in a torrent of screams above him. And then the iron fingers suddenly let loose of his ankles.

Chapter Seven

he instant his legs went free, one ankle was grabbed by a hand with a heavier touch. Squealing like a frightened piglet, Austin frantically kicked his other leg until it, too, was grabbed by a strong, warm set of fingers.

"Hol' still, Massa Austin, it's me!" a voice called down to him.

"Help me, Henry-James!" Austin screamed. "Help me!"

But he wasn't sure he could be heard over the commotion above. Somebody was squalling even louder than he was, words that made no sense beyond "Owww!"

"Crawl up the wall, Massa Austin!" Henry-James shouted.

Austin pawed at the stones with his hands and felt himself being pulled upward. He helped, palming the wall in a frenzy until he bent over at the waist and fell back into Henry-James's arms. The sun shined down on his pulsing face, and he gulped for air.

"I don't think *he'll* be back for a while," he heard Charlotte say.

Austin rocked to his feet and looked behind him. Narvel was limping away like a wounded rabbit, folded in half.

"What happened?" Austin said.

Charlotte grinned over his head at Henry-James, who was

showing his gap in a smile of his own.

"While you were down there squalling," Lottie said, "I sent Jefferson to get somebody—"

"And I was 'bout to grab you and break that boy's leg," Henry-James put in. "But I looks at Miz Lottie and she just a-shakin' her head—"

"There's no point in Henry-James getting in trouble if he doesn't have to," Charlotte said. "I gave him a sign and then I used his trick and Henry-James grabbed you just as Narvel let go."

"What trick?" Austin said.

Charlotte shrugged her ruffled shoulders. "I got him with my knee, just like he did to Henry-James in the wrestling match."

Austin stared at her, and then he started to laugh—big, relieved guffaws that felt better than any he'd ever laughed.

"I wouldn't be laughin' if'n I was you, Massa Austin," Henry-James said, trying unsuccessfully to scowl. "Miz Lottie done save your life!"

"Austin! Oh, thank God!"

It was Sally Hutchinson, hurrying white-faced from the barn-yard with Ria and Jefferson on her heels. She reached Austin with her hands already out to examine his every bone.

"Jefferson said that boy with the 'watermelon head' was holding you upside down in the well!"

"He was," Austin said. He shrank away as she felt his head, only to have the checkup taken over by Ria. He stood impatiently still as she continued the examination. "But Charlotte and Henry-James saved me."

"What on earth happened?" his mother said.

"That's what I want to know," said Uncle Drayton. "And I am going to find out."

He was taking big strides toward them from the other side of the fence. He vaulted lightly over it. Behind him, Micah Guthrie did the same. Narvel sagged against the post with a face the color of porridge and bored his eyes into all of them. Austin muffled a smile with his hand. Charlotte surely had done the boy in.

"Which one was it, Narvel?" Micah Guthrie said in his clenched-up voice. "Which one of them kicked you in the gut?"

Narvel pointed straight at Henry-James. "That one there!" he said. "He's the one did it!"

"No!" Austin cried. "He's lying!"

"You saw, Austin?" Uncle Drayton said.

Austin shook his head wildly. "No—"

"Then hush up, would you, please? I don't have time to haggle over this all day." He turned sharply to Henry-James. "Tell me the truth, boy, and you know you'd better. Did you or did you not drive your knee into this boy's innards?"

"What are you askin' him for?" Micah said. "You know he done it—to get back at Narvel for outsmartin' him in the rasslin' match!"

"I want the answer from him," Uncle Drayton said. He flashed his eyes at Henry-James. "Answer me, boy."

Austin licked his lips. This was going to be perfect. Narvel was going to get his comeuppance, and Henry-James was going to give it to him—with Uncle Drayton's permission.

Henry-James looked respectfully into his master's chest and made his face blank as a wall. "Yes, Marse Drayton," he said. "I'm the one done it."

Austin's mouth flew open, but in the same instant, Henry-James flicked his eyes up and caught Austin's gaze. *Hush up, Massa Austin*, his dark look said. *Please don't say a word.*

Micah gave a satisfied grunt. Narvel's eyes glittered with delight.

Why did you do that, Henry-James? Austin screamed in his head. He searched frantically for Charlotte's eyes. She was staring at her shoe tops and blinking hard. She looked as if she had just kicked *Henry-James* in the stomach.

"It seems you were right, Guthrie," Uncle Drayton said crisply. "Thank you for bringing this to my attention."

"Whatcha gonna do about it?" Micah said between his teeth.

"Whatever I see fit," Uncle Drayton said. "Now if you'll excuse me."

Micah Guthrie frowned, though not as viciously as Narvel was glowering from the fence. *He wanted to see a whipping*, Austin thought angrily. And then his breath caught in his throat. Were he and Charlotte and the rest of them going to see one?

"Drayton, there is more to this than you're hearing," Mother said as the Guthries walked away.

"Were you here?" Uncle Drayton said.

"No, but Jefferson came and told me that Narvel was holding Austin over the well upside down! Henry-James was only trying to save him."

"I beg your pardon, sister," he said. His voice sliced the air. "I have far more important things on my mind right now than the pranks and problems of four children who always seem to have them." Once again he turned sharply to Henry-James. Austin held his breath until he thought his brain would burst.

"Let me say this. One more altercation with Narvel Guthrie, and it will be your turn to see what it's like to be whipped by a white man." He jabbed a thumb into his own chest. *"This* white man. Now you come on along with me. You have work to do."

He strode back toward the Big House, swinging his arms. Henry-James dutifully followed without looking back.

Austin stared after them with his chest heaving. *I used to think Uncle Drayton was handsome*, he thought. *How could I ever have thought that? He's as ugly as Micah Guthrie.*

"I don't understand why you didn't tell him Charlotte did it!" Austin said later that evening.

He and Charlotte were sitting at Daddy Elias's feet in the

cabin on Slave Street. Henry-James was stirring a pot of pork and beans over the fire.

"Ain't no use her gettin' in trouble with her daddy."

"Why would she get in trouble?" Austin cried. "She was trying to save me from being dropped down the well, and so were you! That whining little coward Narvel is the one who should be in trouble, and he gets away free every time!"

"That's 'cause he smarter than you think, Massa Austin," Henry-James said. "All I be thinkin' 'bout while I'm standin' there is how he gonna twist it all 'round so Miz Lottie look like the devil hisself."

"He would, too, wouldn't he?" Austin said. He jerked his knees up to his chest and hugged them. "I know I'm not supposed to say this, but I think I hate Narvel!"

"Mmmm-mmmm," Daddy Elias said.

Austin stared miserably at his knees.

"Don't worry yourself none about it, Massa Austin," Henry-James said. He spooned some hog fat out of the pot and poured it over a piece of cornbread. "I didn't get no whuppin' and I ain't goin' to neither."

"It still isn't fair. I want Narvel to get *his* whipping."

"Let me see your eyes, Massa Austin," Daddy Elias said.

Austin looked at him in surprise. "Why? What's wrong with them?"

"Mmmm-mmmm, just as I thought." Daddy Elias nodded and rocked, his mouth held softly in its spoon-shaped smile. "I reckon you didn't know you got you a beam in your eye, Massa Austin."

Austin blinked furiously. "A beam? What do you mean? I don't have anything in my eye!"

"Maybe you can't feel it, maybe you can't even see it, but Brother Matthew, he know about that beam."

"Matthew in the Bible?" Charlotte said. "Are you going to tell us a story?"

"No, I jus' tellin' Massa Austin not to worry none 'bout the mote in that white boy's eye till he take care o' that beam he totin' around."

"I don't understand," Austin said. His mind was spinning, and he was getting annoyed. It wasn't often he didn't understand something.

"You go in the Good Book and ask Brother Matthew," Daddy Elias said. He eyed the plate Henry-James put in his lap. " 'Cause right now I got to eat my beans and my cracklin' bread."

Austin frowned and poked a finger at his eye, but there was nothing there.

"I think I know what you mean," Charlotte said to Daddy Elias. "You think we shouldn't worry about that old nasty Narvel and we should just worry about Henry-James."

"You think Massa Narvel such a nasty boy, Miz Lottie?" Daddy Elias said as he chewed toothlessly.

"I do!" Charlotte said. "He's tried to hurt my two best friends."

"I ain't never knowed a boy, black or white, didn't act off'n his own heart."

"So he has a nasty heart," Austin said.

"A nasty heart somebody done give him." Daddy Elias closed his eyes and sniffed a shell full of beans and pork with pleasure before he let it slide into his mouth.

"Who gave it to him?" Austin said impatiently.

Daddy Elias just enjoyed another mouthful of his supper and slowly shook his head. "I reckon you'll find out, Massa Austin. You a smart boy with Jesus in your heart. Yes, I reckon you'll figure that out jus' fine."

It rained for almost two days. The rain was good for the soil, Uncle Drayton said, but it kept the slaves from working the fields. It also kept the Guthries away, and that didn't make the children unhappy. But it didn't erase thoughts of Nasty Narvel from Austin's mind.

Why can't Daddy Elias just tell me what he means? he asked grumpily Saturday night as he was saying his prayers in the dark. *Why does he make me try to figure out what a mote in Narvel's eye and a beam in mine means?*

Jesus, what's a mote?

He didn't have to wait long to find out. The next day as he sat in his dark blue velvet suit between his mother and Jefferson at St. Paul's church, he was startled to hear those very words come out of Reverend Pullens' mouth.

" 'Wilt thou say to thy brother, Let me pull out the mote out of thine eye; and behold, a beam is in thine own eye?' " he read from the big Bible on the pulpit. " 'Thou hypocrite!' "

Now that was a word he'd never heard before. Austin leaned close to his mother. "What's a hypocrite?" he whispered.

She put her lips next to his ear. "It's a person who says he believes in Jesus but doesn't act that way," she said.

Austin nodded thoughtfully. Then Daddy Elias *was* talking about Narvel—and Uncle Drayton, too. He felt his chest slowly swell. Maybe Uncle Drayton said he was a Christian and then turned around and treated people like they were his belongings— and maybe Narvel claimed he was being abused when he was the one doing it—but not him, not Austin.

Jesus is my friend, Austin thought, the way Daddy Elias had taught him. *And that's the way I act.*

He sat up straight in the seat and slanted a glance down at his uncle and aunt. *I'm sure glad I'm not like them.*

But somehow, that didn't make things any easier. Narvel Guthrie was going after Henry-James like it was his job. And Austin had to admit, he was crafty about it.

On Monday while Narvel and Henry-James were both on trash gang in the morning, picking up all the garbage and debris in the fields, Bogie suddenly began to yelp and dance around like a mad dog. Someone had attached a crab to his tail. It wasn't hard to guess who.

On Tuesday, Henry-James found a pig dropping in his dinner bucket. As Austin and Charlotte ran to the kitchen building to get him something else to eat, they spotted Narvel snickering behind a tree.

On Wednesday while Henry-James led the singing during a dike repair job, Narvel went behind him and imitated him in a high-pitched, girlish voice.

Every evening, Henry-James told them about Narvel's pranks while he or Polly fixed Daddy Elias's supper in the cabin, and every night Jefferson said, "Did you get him back, Henry-James?"

And every night Henry-James said, "No sirree. I done been warned. I don't want no whuppin'. I just stands there and takes it."

"That's because you aren't a hypocrite and Narvel is," Austin said on Wednesday night.

He looked at Daddy Elias for his nod. But the light of approval didn't flicker in the old man's eyes. He just looked at Austin and rocked.

"Isn't that right?" Austin said.

"I don't know 'bout them big words, Massa Austin," he said. "I only knows what the good Lord tell me."

"Me, too," Austin said happily.

But he didn't stay happy for long. The next day, he, Charlotte, Jefferson, Polly, Tot, and Bogie went to meet Henry-James for dinner. It was a glorious, crisp fall day, and Aunt Olivia was all in a dither because Uncle Drayton was having guests for the afternoon meal, so she shooed the children off to have a picnic.

They tore off across the barnyard toward the shops where Henry-James was waiting for the tanner to finish a new pair of boots for Uncle Drayton. Polly and Tot carried the food basket between them with Jefferson hopping up and down, trying to peek in. Austin was pumping to keep up with Charlotte.

"We thought there weren't going to be any more picnics this year!" he said, huffing and puffing.

"This will make Henry-James happy," Charlotte said. "Nasty Narvel is making him miserable. He needs some cheering up."

Henry-James's face did light up when he saw them, and after dropping off the boots to a frantic Aunt Olivia, who was trying to "gussy Drayton up" for his visitors, he led the way to his favorite spot in the trees near Rice Mill Pond. Even Aunt Olivia's final screeching words—"Now you have yourself back here and in your uniform by the time those gentlemen arrive, boy!"—didn't bother them. They spread out the picnic cloth and commenced to devouring Josephine's treats with Polly presiding.

"Are you practicing to be a wife?" Austin asked her as she handed out peppermint cakes.

She looked at him cautiously and seemed to decide he wasn't picking on her. "Yes," she said. "You just wait—Garrison McCloud will be back."

"I don't care about him," Charlotte said. "I just wish Kady would come back out. I miss her."

"Is she in jail?" Jefferson asked.

"Hush up, shrimp," Austin said. "Let's change the subject."

"I sure 'nuff can't wait for Saturday," Henry-James said.

"What's happening Saturday?" Polly said, pouring Austin another glass of milk and looking every bit the plantation mistress.

"I gets the afternoon off and I'm a-goin' huntin'," Henry-James said.

"Oh." Polly sniffed disdainfully. "I don't think I'd like that."

"I would!" Austin said.

"Why don't you come on and go with me then, Massa Austin? You always sayin' you want to know 'bout them things."

"That would be . . . amazing!" Austin said. He got up on his knees so fast that Bogie turned from the soup bone he was chewing and gave him a long look. "I've read all about it, of course. What are we after?"

"Anything we can trap. Rabbit, squirrel, coon, maybe possum. Coon—now that's better eatin' than possum."

"It all sounds wretched to me!" Polly said. Tot nodded enthusiastically and handed her a napkin. Polly stared at it blankly for a minute before she took it and patted her brow.

"Not if it's cooked up fine, Miz Polly," Henry-James said. "When me and Massa Austin is done, you come on down to the cabin, and I show you how to cook up a coon stew make your mouth water."

"Do you think a wealthy man would want a wife that knew how to make coon stew?" Polly said.

But a shadow passed over Henry-James's face.

"What's the matter?" Charlotte said.

He shook his head. "Ain't nothin', Miz Lottie."

But Austin followed his gaze off into the trees. He caught a glimpse of something red disappearing among the trunks.

"What do you think that was?" Austin said.

Still Henry-James shook his head. "Ain't nothin'. Ain't nothin' at all."

"You'd better get back, Henry-James," Charlotte said. "You'll be in trouble if you're late."

"I'll walk to the Big House with you," Austin said, scrambling up. "Just in case, you know."

As soon as they were out of earshot of the rest of the picnickers, Austin whispered, "You don't think that was Narvel Guthrie spying on us, do you?"

"Sure 'nuff was, Massa Austin," Henry-James whispered back. "But I don't want no more trouble from that white boy." He pursed his lips. "What I ever done to him, Massa Austin?"

"You're better than him and he's jealous, that's all there is to it," Austin said. "You're so good, you don't even tell on him when he does mean stuff to you—every day!"

"Wouldn't do me no good," Henry-James said as they fell in among the fiery-colored trees. " 'Sides, it ain't worth it, me gettin' in trouble jus' for my own self. Now, if'n you or Miz Lottie or Massa Jefferson needs me—now that there is somethin' else again."

Austin straightened his shoulders and grinned up at Henry-James. Suddenly, Austin's right foot sank, and he felt a tug at his leg.

A second later he was swinging upside down from an oak limb by his ankle.

Chapter Eight

The ground spun dizzily below him as Austin hung like a rag doll by one leg.

"What happened?" he screamed. It felt like he was living a nightmare all over again.

"You done stepped into a trap, Massa Austin!" Henry-James cried. "You hangin' by a rope that won't quit!"

Austin could already feel it cutting into his ankle. Having someone hold on with his fingers was one thing, but this hurt. This time he could see the hard ground far beneath him, and it made his heart slam against the inside of his chest.

"Can you get me down?" he said.

"I'm sure 'nuff gonna try."

Henry-James was already halfway up the trunk of the big live oak. Austin tried to swallow, but it was hard upside down. His head was pounding even harder than it had when he was hanging in the well.

"Can you hurry?" Austin called out.

"That's jus' what I's doin'. Can you curl yourself up, Massa Austin? Your head lookin' mighty red."

Austin pulled his free leg against the tied one and then tried to pull his head toward his belly button, which was by now exposed to the woods. His head stopped hammering, but he could only stay that way for a minute. His muscles started to shake, and he swung back down.

Above, he heard Henry-James on a limb.

"Can you get it untied?" Austin called. It felt like his voice was coming out his nose.

"This some kind of complicated contraption up here, Massa Austin," Henry-James said. "But I get you out."

"Contraption?" Austin said. If he hadn't felt like his face was going to burst open, he'd have found that interesting.

"Try curlin' yourself up one more time, Massa Austin," Henry-James said. "This gonna take me a while. Good thing you likes to be upside down."

"Not this much!" Austin said. His heart was beating faster, and he was sure any second he was going to throw up the picnic lunch.

"Henry-James?" a tiny voice peeped out. "You out here, Henry-James?"

"Is that you, Mousie?" Austin said. He swung himself around and saw her scurrying along the ground below like a chipmunk. She gave a startled sideways jump and lowered her nervous eyes to the path.

"You ain't seen Henry-James, has you, Massa?" she said.

Austin flung an arm up toward the tree limb, and Henry-James poked his face out of the leaves.

"Oh, my," she said.

She stood there blinking at him for so long that Henry-James gave up and disappeared again.

"No, Henry-James!" she said, the words squealing. "You got to come down and run to the Big House. Missus be lookin' for you, and she 'bout to go plumb crazy!"

It was the most Austin had ever heard Mousie say. He didn't even think she knew that many words. This must be serious.

"Them gentlemens be coming up the river right now in they boat, and she say if'n you ain't there by the time they sets foot on the shore, she gonna tell Marse Drayton for sure!" Mousie stopped to catch her breath. "She say he gon' whup your backside clean off!"

"You have to go, Henry-James!" Austin cried. He curled up again and hung on to his knees with his hands. "This isn't worth getting a whipping for!"

"I ain't gonna leave you here for your insides to turn backwards, Massa Austin!" Henry-James called down.

"Mousie can go get somebody else!" Austin said. "Go on, now, hurry!"

Henry-James pushed his face back out of the leaves and looked down at Austin. "Look at that, Massa Austin," he said. He pointed at Austin's tied ankle. "You bleedin' bad from that there rope. I ain't goin' nowhere till I gets you down, and I don't care if'n Marse Drayton beat me from now to Sunday." He pulled back into the leaves again.

Austin couldn't hold himself upright any longer, and he rolled back down. Mousie was still there, wringing her little paws.

"What I'm gonna do, Massa?" she said. "Missus tell me don't come back without that boy!"

"You ain't goin' back without me!" Henry-James cried suddenly. "I done got this here thing figured out!"

Austin took a breath and forced himself to curl up again. His stomach muscles were aching, his head was throbbing, and he was tasting peppermint cakes, which were nowhere near as good the second time. Henry-James slapped the leaves aside.

"You got to hang down one more time, Massa Austin," Henry-James said, "so's you can keep yourself from banging into this here tree while I pulls you on up."

"How are you going to do that? Are you that strong?"

"I done figured out how to use this crank somebody put in

here. You just take care yourself and I have you rightside up 'fore you can say *Virginiana quinces*."

Austin felt a laugh bubble up—well, down—his throat. He let himself fall down and stuck out his hands to push away from the rough tree trunk. In less than a minute, Henry-James was hauling him right onto the branch. He sat up and watched the world do a sickening spin.

"Now if'n you don' mind, Massa Austin, I gots to go."

Mousie nodded and darted off toward the Big House.

"I just hope I can get into them fancy clothes and be at the door 'fore them gentlemens gets there," Henry-James said.

Austin peered curiously at the crank-and-rope contraption someone had taken a lot of trouble to nail to the tree. "This looks like an old pulley from a well," he said. "Now how did they rig it up so a person would trip?"

"I don't know nothin' 'bout that. All I knows is, I's 'bout to get me a whuppin'.'"

Henry-James was already shinnying down the tree, and Austin followed him, his head still pounding and his ankle beginning to throb.

"I'm going with you, Henry-James," he said. "I'll explain it all to Uncle Drayton."

"He ain't gonna listen," Henry-James said as he jumped to the ground and put a hand up to help Austin.

They headed toward the Big House, and Austin limped to keep up. "He's listened to me before," he said.

"He ain't never had his heart heavy as it is now. He got so many troubles on his mind, he can't even listen to hisself."

"He's going to listen to me," Austin said stubbornly. "I'll take the whipping myself if I have to."

Henry-James grunted and picked up the pace.

"Anyway, I already have a plan," Austin said. "You go change into your uniform while I go to the river side of the house and stall Uncle Drayton's visitors before they get to the front door. I'll think of something to say."

"I's sure you will, Massa Austin," Henry-James said. His voice sounded a little more hopeful.

But all hope faded when they broke out of the trees. The men were already out of the boat and standing on the velvety grass "steps" that led from the Ashley River to the front of the mansion.

And Uncle Drayton was there with them.

Henry-James froze and his arms flew out in panic.

"It's all right," Austin said. "Just go put your uniform on and gussy yourself up, and I'll go down and explain everything to Uncle Drayton."

"I don' know, Massa Austin—"

"I promise it'll be all right. *Go!*"

Henry-James gave Austin one last long, wide-eyed look before he turned on a bare heel and took off for the kitchen building, where his uniform was kept. Austin hobbled toward the three men on the lawn. His ankle was shooting pains up his leg, but that, he decided, couldn't hurt as much as a whip would across Henry-James's bare back.

He slowed down and groaned to himself.

The two men standing with Uncle Drayton were Virgil Rhett and Lawson Chesnut.

The Fire Eaters, he thought with a moan. *Why don't they just leave Uncle Drayton alone?*

It didn't matter who was there, though. Henry-James was more important. Austin had to get down there and explain all this before Uncle Drayton discovered his body slave wasn't waiting at the front door.

Austin was still too far away to see their faces clearly, but their words were loud enough to be heard all the way to Slave Street.

"You are a murderer, Drayton Ravenal!" Virgil Rhett was shrieking.

"How on earth do you figure me for a murderer? Who's being killed?"

"You are standing by while the North persecutes the South!"

"If your daughter were being strangled by a stranger," Mr. Chesnut shouted, "you wouldn't just stand there and let it happen. You'd count yourself worse than the killer if you did!"

"But I don't see anybody dying!" Austin heard his uncle say as he drew closer.

"Oh, but they will!" cried Mr. Rhett. "The very minute Abraham Lincoln is elected next week, the South will begin to fade away like a dried-up cornstalk!"

"And we're going to hold you responsible, Ravenal!"

Austin came to a stop at the corner of the house and gnawed at his fingernail. This wasn't a good time to burst in on the conversation. Rhett and Chesnut were red-faced and pacing. Austin knew if he were closer, he'd be able to see Mr. Chesnut's nostrils flaring wide enough to drive a buggy through and Mr. Rhett's caterpillar eyebrows tying up in knots. Even Uncle Drayton was losing his temper. His tan face was beet-red all the way up to the roots of his hair.

Behind Austin, Henry-James huffed to a halt, breathing like a locomotive and buttoning the gold buttons on his vest.

"It's them men again, Massa Austin," Henry-James whispered. "They bring trouble every time."

Austin nodded. "That's why I'm waiting." He felt a smile slowly spread across his face. "Hey, I know! You just go stand at the front door like you've been there all the time! They could be arguing for days!"

Henry-James furrowed his brow for a second, and then he nodded. "You right, Massa Austin. Woo, Lordy, this here was a close one!"

Austin gave him a gentle shove toward the front porch. When he turned toward the trio on the lawn again, the voices were climbing—and Virgil Rhett was holding his fist up to his chin.

"I want nothing to do with your violent vision!" Uncle Drayton shouted at him.

"You don't have any choice, Ravenal, unless you want to just stand there and take it!" Chesnut shouted back. He was so agitated that he could hardly breathe, and his voice wheezed out like an old goat's bleat. "And you're too much of a man of honor to do that—you've said it yourself a thousand times!"

"Let's see if he means it, then!" Virgil Rhett cried.

The fist that he'd held taut in front of his chin snapped out and caught Uncle Drayton square in the jaw. His face was thrown sideways. When he looked back, bewildered, Virgil Rhett was ready with another punch, which he delivered to Drayton's nose. Uncle Drayton stumbled back and caught himself halfway to the ground. Before he could right himself, Rhett was towering over him, fist pulled back, and Chesnut was pulling off his jacket.

Austin was paralyzed . . . but Henry-James wasn't. He shot down the grassy steps from the front porch, feet kicking out behind him, black face set. As Austin watched, rooted to the ground, the slave boy hurled himself onto Virgil Rhett's back and toppled him off balance. Reaching down, he grabbed the tall man's leg and pulled it out from under him, dropping them both to the ground.

They rolled once with Henry-James coming out on top. He left Virgil Rhett on the ground and ran to Uncle Drayton's side. Drayton was standing with his arms stuck out like sticks, as astonished as everyone else.

Austin was the first to recover.

"Uncle Drayton!" he shouted as he half-ran, half-hopped-on-one-foot. "I saw it all! Henry-James was trying to save you!"

Chesnut reached out importantly and grabbed Austin's shoulder. Austin jerked it away and kept his eyes on his uncle, who was still staring about him. Henry-James stood right beside him, head down. Only Virgil Rhett stayed on the ground. He was inspecting his limbs as if he'd just been beaten to a pulp.

"Henry-James doesn't deserve a whipping, Uncle Drayton!" Austin said. "He only jumped on Mr. Rhett because he was going to hit you again."

"Miserable little cuffee!" Rhett cried. "I think he broke my leg!"

"I'm sure he did nothin' of the kind," Uncle Drayton said tightly, "though heaven knows you deserve that and more! What do you mean, coming onto my land and attacking me!"

"Because if you aren't with us, you're against us!" Chesnut wheezed. "You're the enemy—"

"And this is how it's going to be once the South secedes without you, Ravenal," Rhett said. He pulled himself gingerly from the ground and brushed off his black frock coat. "You'll be considered a traitor to your homeland. This is merely a taste of what your life is going to be like."

"We agreed last summer at Flat Rock that there was going to be no violence—"

"I never agreed to stand by and let you wreck the cause!"

"Neither did I," Chesnut put in, poking a thick finger in the air. "And you're surely doing it, Mr. Ravenal. You can't even keep your darkies under control! First you educate them. Then you allow them to attack their betters like rabid dogs!"

Austin couldn't keep his mouth shut any longer. "You're the rabid dog!" he cried. "You punched Uncle Drayton for no reason!"

Chesnut's nostrils flared nearly to his side whiskers. "You see!" he said, stabbing his forefinger at Austin. "Your whole plantation is out of control. I have children insulting me now!"

"Austin!" Uncle Drayton said sharply. "Go to the house."

"But you—"

"Go—and find Ria. Your ankle is bleeding."

Austin didn't move—until Uncle Drayton said, "Henry-James,

carry him in, and then stay there. I will deal with you later."

"Deal with him?" Austin cried. "But he didn't do anything wrong!"

"Go!"

There was no use arguing with Uncle Drayton when he brought out a full section of trumpets. But it wasn't fear that made Austin climb up onto Henry-James's back and trot with him off to the house without a word. It was anger.

"I don't see why you even jumped in there and saved him from getting hurt," Austin said when they were safely out of hearing inside the front door. "The way he treats you, I'd have let him be beaten up."

Henry-James headed wordlessly to the steps like a horse.

"You didn't have to do that, you know," Austin raved on. "You could have just stood there and said you were waiting for Uncle Drayton to give you permission to 'attack your social better'."

Henry-James stopped on the third step and looked at Austin over his shoulder. "I couldn't do that, Massa Austin. It wouldn'ta been right."

"But he's such a hypocrite! He'll take a beating before he'll change his mind about secession because he wants to be 'honorable.' But then he'll turn around and punish you for trying to save somebody's life without permission because it's against the rules!"

"What you talkin' 'bout—'hypocrite'? What's that?"

Henry-James trudged on up the steps with Austin hanging on.

"It's a person who says he believes in Jesus but does things Jesus wouldn't like," Austin said.

Henry-James grunted. "I thought it was another one of them names for a tree."

While Ria wrapped Austin's ankle, the two boys waited for Uncle Drayton to come in and "deal with" Henry-James. Henry-James paced the floor of the kitchen building. Austin made plans in his head.

I won't let him give Henry-James a whipping, that's for sure, he thought fiercely. *I don't care how heavy his heart is! I'm gonna show him what a hypocrite is.*

But Uncle Drayton never came looking for his slave boy at all. As Rhett and Chesnut paddled off up the river like madmen, Drayton stormed into the Big House and locked himself in the library.

"It's like hearing the thunder and waiting for the lightning to come," Austin said that night at supper in his mother's room.

"If there was going to be lightning, we would have seen it by now," Mother said. "I know Drayton—he burns up his anger fast and then sits in his smoldering ashes for days."

"Then you don't think he's going to punish Henry-James?" Austin said.

Mother shook her head. "Look how many chances he's given him. He blows a lot of smoke, but I don't really think he wants to whip him at all."

Austin grinned. "Then Henry-James and I can still go hunting on Saturday. Are you coming, Lottie?"

Charlotte shook her head. "I don't like seeing those little animals get caught in those traps," she said.

"That's Henry-James's dinner, though," Austin said.

"I'd rather give him mine. Besides—" she plucked restlessly at the sleeves of her striped dress "—I'm afraid to go. I wish you wouldn't either."

"Why is that, honey?" Mother said.

"Because too many awful things have been happening. Henry-James got kicked in the stomach. Nasty Narvel held Austin over the well. And I just know it was him who set that trap in the tree. Kady says he has a good side, but—"

"Not a chance," Austin said, sweeping it all away with his hand. "He isn't smart enough to figure out something like that."

"Who else is?" Polly said. "You're the only one I know who's smart enough to think that up. I doubt you'd do it to yourself."

"I don't care," Austin said. "Nothing is going to keep us from going hunting and having an *amazing* time."

"I'm glad to hear you talk like that, my love," Mother said. "All I've been hearing lately is crying and shouting and blaming and accusing. It's nice to hear some excitement. You just hang on to that."

And Austin did. It seemed to take three weeks for Saturday to arrive, and with each hour his expectation grew like Josephine's bread dough. When he wasn't talking about it to whomever would sit still and listen—mostly Bogie—he was reading about coons and possums and traps.

"I will be so glad when this hunting trip is over," Polly said Saturday morning at breakfast in the drawing room. "You're driving us near to crazy with all this talk."

"I don't think it's going to be over even then," Mother said, eyes twinkling. She sipped at her cocoa. "You know he's going to come back and tell us every detail."

There was a whole symphony of moaning and protesting then, but all of them came out onto the back porch that afternoon to see Austin off when he left in his blue denim shirt and wool trousers tucked into his ankle jackboots. He really wished he had a buckskin coat with long fringes. He'd read that it drained off water when it rained—and it would look so manly.

But it couldn't have looked less like rain as he, Henry-James, and Bogie headed off into the woods. Although there was a chilly early-November breeze, the sun burned warmly through it from a bright blue sky. Austin grinned as he walked jauntily beside Henry-James—who was looking pretty pleased with himself as well.

"I got me a afternoon off," Henry-James said. "I done picked up the rations for the day in the cellar from missus, and I's free."

"So where are we going first?" Austin said. "You're the boss today."

Henry-James rubbed his broad nose thoughtfully. "I reckon we go on over by the swampland. That's where the best trappin' is this time o' year. What you think, Bogie?"

Bogie seemed to agree. He slurped at both their hands and then bounded ahead into the dense woods of cypress and sweet gum. Henry-James and Austin had to trot to keep up, darting in and out of yellow-green stands of bamboo and tripping over cypress knees nosing their little way out of the ground.

"*Taxodium distichium*," Austin said happily.

Every time Bogie got out of sight, Henry-James would stop and whistle, and Bogie would howl gleefully until they caught up to him again.

"I bet Bogie's the smartest dog in the world," Austin said. It seemed like a day for saying things like that—everything was so perfect.

"I reckon he is," Henry-James agreed as they slowed down to catch their breath. " 'Cept he can't wait to get where he's goin'. We done lost him again."

He stopped and puckered his lips in a whistle. At first there was no answer, except for the high-pitched scream of an eagle from the top of a tall cypress.

Henry-James whistled again. This time they heard a growl, one of Bogie's juicy, angry ones.

"He sees something," Austin said.

Henry-James started to run through the brush toward the sound of Bogie's furious carrying on. And then they heard a sound that cracked the air.

Henry-James stopped dead still.

"What was that?" Austin said.

"That there was a gunshot," Henry-James said. His eyes went wild. "Somebody shootin' a gun out there where Bogie is!"

He took off like a shot himself with Austin on his heels. Both of them were screaming Bogie's name . . . until they crashed into a clearing—and found Bogie lying limp on the ground, eyes closed, chest still.

here was blood trailing down from Bogie's shoulder, and it was fast making a puddle on the ground.

"Bogie!" Henry-James cried. He flung himself on top of the perfectly still dog and lifted up his big head. "Open your eyes! Say somethin' to me, boy!"

"Is he breathing?" Austin said.

Henry-James shook his head against Bogie's wrinkly fur.

"He dead, Massa Austin!" he said. "Somebody done killed him dead!"

Henry-James pulled himself up with a jerk and frantically began scanning the woods with his eyes. The breeze turned cold against Austin's skin.

"What are you gonna do?" Austin said.

"I'm gonna find him."

He made the statement flat and hard, and then he took off into the trees.

"Henry-James!" Austin called after him.

There was no answer but the screaming of the eagle. The sound was chilling in the empty woods. The silence of Bogie was even worse.

Austin stared down at him, and his eyes blurred. He dropped

down on his knees and tucked his fingers in the folds of the dog's skin. It was still warm, the way it was when Austin used him for a pillow while he looked for pictures in the clouds.

"Bogie, please don't be dead," Austin whispered to him.

The eagle screamed again, and Austin twitched. "Stop it!" he shouted up at the bird. "Can't you see he's sleeping?"

But he wasn't sleeping. Austin buried his face in Bogie's loose skin.

"You were the best dog in the world," he said into his fur. "You *were*."

Someone groaned, and Austin's head jerked up.

"Henry-James?" he said.

His heart started to slam. What if it was the dog shooter? What if he came back?

There was another groan—louder this time. Austin stared down at Bogie's body.

"Bogie?" he whispered. "Was that you?"

Bogie didn't open his eyes or bark or even whine. But his shoulder jerked, and again there was a groan. It came from deep inside Bogie somewhere.

Desperately, Austin pushed his face next to Bogie's nose. There was a tiny puff of air, warm against his cold cheek. Then another one.

Austin pulled up the dog's droopy eyelid. A tear slithered down his nose.

"Lordy!" Austin shouted. "You're not dead!"

He looked around wildly and tried to get his thoughts into one pile. *I have to get him back to the plantation. Ria can make him better. I have to tell Henry-James.*

He sat up on his heels and cupped his hands around his mouth. He called five times, but there was no answer. Below him, Bogie gave another pitiful moan.

"I'm gonna get you home, boy," Austin whispered to him.

"You just hang on and I'll get you there."

Austin wrapped his arms around Bogie's middle and tried to lift him, but the big dog was even heavier than he appeared. Austin looked anxiously around for something to carry him in.

If I could make a pouch, I could carry him over my shoulder, he thought as he searched the clearing.

But there was nothing he could use. The puddle of blood by Bogie's shoulder was getting bigger, and Austin's mouth was going dry.

What does Ria do when somebody's bleeding?

Quickly, he took off his denim shirt and wrapped it tightly around Bogie's shoulder. It began to ooze red. *I'll just get him to Ria,* he told himself. *Then it'll be all right.*

The question was, how? The shirt-bandage gave him an idea. With shaking fingers, he slid out of his wool trousers and, standing there in his long flannel underwear, tied the pant legs in a knot. *This would be better if it were a skirt*, he thought. *But this will work. It has to!*

He wrapped the makeshift sling around the middle of Bogie, being careful not to move his bleeding shoulder. Looping the sling over his own shoulder, he got slowly to his feet. Bogie's head flopped one way, his hind legs and tail the other, but his shoulder and ribs hugged firmly up against Austin.

"All right, boy," Austin whispered, "we're going home."

He wasn't sure why he was whispering. It just felt as if talking out loud might break the fragile string that was keeping Bogie alive. He hoped walking wouldn't do it—and he took tiny, gentle steps.

Ten of them and his arm was aching. Austin set down his bundle and stepped over it to the other side. He checked once more to make sure Bogie was still breathing and pulled him onto his other shoulder.

They got 20 steps this time.

This is going to take all night, Austin thought. His throat closed in on threatening tears. *I've read when people bleed too much they—*

"Henry-James!" he cried out. "Where are you? Bogie's alive! Come help me!"

"Austin!" someone else called out.

It was Charlotte.

As if her voice were a tonic, Austin took off at a run, with Bogie bouncing against him. Charlotte shot out from behind a tree and stopped, her eyes startled into fear.

"What happened?" she said. "We heard a shot."

Polly plowed in behind her and at once plastered her hands over her mouth. Tot let out a scream.

"Is he dead?" Charlotte asked.

Polly blinked at Austin. "Where are your clothes?"

"He isn't dead," Austin said. "Somebody shot him, but he didn't die. But we have to get him to Ria or I'm afraid he's going to."

"Where's Henry-James?" Charlotte said.

"He ran off to find whoever did it. He thought Bogie was dead. But you have to help me!"

Polly was eyeing the sling. "You need something bigger than that," she said.

"Here," Charlotte said. She pulled up the hem of her skirt. "Use my dress."

"Charlotte Anne, don't you dare take your clothes off in the woods!" Polly cried.

Tot pointed at Austin.

"I know he did," Polly said, "but that's different."

"What about Tot's apron?" Austin said.

Tot looked down, stricken, at her starched white apron. Polly only gave it a brief glance.

"Take it off, Tot," she said briskly.

Tot looked as if she would rather spit out her teeth one by one. But Polly gave her a hard poke, and she untied the strings. Polly presented it to Austin with a flourish.

Together, Tot, Polly, and Austin retied the sling, using both the trousers and the apron, while Charlotte stroked Bogie's head and talked to him. This time when they lifted him up, his head and hind legs stayed inside like a baby in a cradle. Austin took the front end and Tot the back, so he was lighter to carry now. Charlotte stayed where she could keep checking his breathing, and Polly led the way, head high and arms swinging.

"I think a man would want a woman who could carry herself well in a crisis," she said over her shoulder.

Ria was hanging out her wash on the cabin porch when they reached Slave Street with their burden.

"Good Lordy," she said. "Take him in an' put him in front of the fire."

They did, and Austin untied the sling. Ria leaned over Bogie's shoulder.

"He done been shot!" she said. Her head snapped up. "Where's Henry-James?"

Austin explained while Charlotte ran for a pan of water, Daddy Elias lit a tallow candle, and Tot examined her bloody apron and whimpered.

"You can make him well, can't you?" Austin said. "I mean, if anyone can, it's you. You've worked a miracle on my mother. I could help. I've read some about gunshot wounds. You have to get the bullet out first and—"

"I knows what to do, Massa Austin," Ria said calmly. She held up two bloody fingers with a marble-sized ball between them. "I reckon that missed killin' him by a angel's eyelash."

Charlotte arrived with the water, and she and Austin both helped wash Bogie's wound and bandage it. He looked clean and comfortable lying by the fire, but still he didn't open his eyes.

"He's gonna be all right now, right?" Austin asked.

Ria drew her mouth into a line. "Only time gonna tell," she said.

"And the Good Lord."

Austin looked at Daddy Elias. He was sure the old man's eyes were moist. Charlotte went over and put her head in his lap.

"We just have to pray, that's all," Austin said. "I'm pretty sure Jesus must like dogs. Don't you think?"

He wasn't sure what he was saying. It just felt better to talk. Too many scary ideas came when there was silence.

Polly stood up and sighed. "We'd better all get up to the Big House," she said. "We were supposed to come back and tell Mama what the shot was we heard."

"I'm not leaving Bogie," Austin said.

" 'Scuse me for sayin'," Ria said, "but I wish you would go on now, Massa Austin. If'n missus find out you here when you s'pose to be there, we the ones gets in trouble."

Austin nodded and got up. *I'm tired of Aunt Olivia*, he thought. *And I'm tired of trouble.*

Supper was on the table when they arrived, and Mother, Drayton, Olivia, and even Kady were there. The ham biscuits, hoppin' John, and field peas steamed uneaten in their bowls.

Aunt Olivia immediately threw her napkin across her mouth. "Austin Hutchinson, what do you mean coming into this dining room in your drawers!"

"He was on a mission of mercy, Mama," Polly said primly. "Bogie was shot and we had to carry him home."

The napkin went to Aunt Olivia's chest, and she raised her eyes to the ceiling. "Thank the Lord it was only the dog."

Austin scowled. "He's hurt bad!"

"Then they ought to just put him down," Uncle Drayton said. "If he lives, he'll probably never be the same."

Kady's fork clattered to her plate. "We are not talking about one of your hunting hounds, Daddy. This is a pet. He's all Henry-James has."

Uncle Drayton's face clouded. "And where is the boy? I don't want to go up to a cold room after supper."

Austin clamped his lips together doggedly. *He's not going to get it out of me*, he thought. *This is one time I know to keep my mouth shut.*

Aunt Olivia gave a dramatic sigh. "I'm quite weary of this talk about animals at my table. Sit down, all of you—except you, Austin. I will not allow a half-naked boy in the dining room."

Austin was more than happy to leave. Once upstairs, he was tempted not to go back down at all. He wasn't hungry, not after seeing Bogie the way he was. He looked out the window toward Slave Street.

I could sleep on the floor with him, and I'd give him water every hour.

"Where is everybody?"

Austin turned to see Jefferson standing in their bedroom doorway, face smeared with the molasses he must have just finished. Austin got down on his knees and held out his arms. Jefferson narrowed his blue eyes suspiciously.

"What do you want?" he said.

"Nothing," Austin said. "I just want you to come here. I want to tell you something."

Jefferson took a step backward. "Tell me from here," he said. "Why do you look like that?"

Austin gave up and rocked back on his knees. "Bogie got shot today," he said. "But Ria's gonna fix him—I know she will—and we're all gonna pray hard—and Henry-James isn't going to get in trouble—and Uncle Drayton isn't going to make him put him down—and everything is gonna be all right—it has to be—because we're the winners—we aren't hypocrites!"

"Austin?" Jefferson said. His blue eyes drooped. "If everything is gonna be all right, why are you crying?"

"I don't know," Austin blubbered. And he didn't.

Jefferson came over and slung a pudgy arm around his shoulder. Below, there was a banging on the front door. Voices curled up from the front hallway as the door was opened. One belonged to Barnabas Brown. The other growl was Irvin Ullmann's.

"It's the Patty Rollers!" Austin whispered to Jefferson.

They both dove for the hall and peered over the banister. The two scraggly men stood looking smug, with Henry-James between them.

"He's bleeding!" Jefferson cried.

Austin put his hand over Jefferson's mouth and looked for himself. Henry-James was bleeding, from his nose, as if someone had slapped him across the face with an open hand. But seeing him with his hands tied behind his back was even worse. Proud, bright Henry-James looked so ashamed. Austin took two steps down to untie him, but the crisp footsteps of Uncle Drayton from the dining room stopped him.

"You've found him then," Uncle Drayton said coldly. "Where was he?"

"Clear down the road, 'bout a half mile off your property, Mr. Ravenal," Barnabas said. His voice whined from out of his thin beard. "He was just a-screamin' his head off."

There was a flurry of dresses behind Uncle Drayton, and the rest of the family appeared in the hallway. Austin saw Charlotte startle like she'd been burnt with a pine knot. Kady put an arm around her.

"Looks to me like he was tryin' to run away," Irvin growled.

"That would explain why he was screaming and drawing attention to himself," Kady said dryly.

"He was just looking for the person who shot his dog," Polly said.

"And look at that!" Austin cried. "They've already hit him—and tied him up!"

"Enough!"

Uncle Drayton's arms flew out, and the room was stung into silence.

"He didn't have no pass," Irvin grumbled.

"I know that!"

Irvin ran his hand over his balding head and stared out from under his scowling brow.

"I thank you for bringing my property back," Uncle Drayton said, holding his face stiff. "I will handle it from here."

Barnabas cleared his throat and began to shuffle. His fingers were twitching.

"You'll get your money," Uncle Drayton snapped. "Go wait in the library."

The two men sent up a cloud of dust as they hurried through the doorway under the stairs. Aunt Olivia put one hand to her lips as she watched them go and stuck out her other hand to Mousie, who was ready with the hanky.

"I hope they don't sit down on those chairs," Austin heard his aunt murmur.

"You!" Uncle Drayton said. His voice was rising again, and he was pointing at Henry-James. Jefferson cowered behind Austin's pant leg. "Go find yourself a barrel, boy!"

"Daddy, you aren't really going to whip him!" Kady said. "He was doing what any normal person would do. He was trying to find out who shot his dog!"

"This boy is not 'any normal person'," Uncle Drayton snapped at her. "He is my body slave, and he is therefore not allowed to leave this property without written permission from me."

"You're talking about your precious Slave Code. I'm talking about a human being!"

"It isn't enough that I am allowing you to educate them!"

Uncle Drayton flared back at her. "Now you want me to let them do just as they please, when they please!"

"I want you to think about their feelings!"

"Feelings do not provide that dress you have on, Kady Sarah, or that meal you just ate! If I allow my darkies to run out of control, we will all run naked and starve to death!"

Aunt Olivia gasped as if that tragedy were going to occur within the moment. If Austin hadn't been ready to fly over the stair rail and into Uncle Drayton's face, he would have rolled his eyes at Charlotte. As it was, she was staring only at Henry-James, her golden-brown eyes as liquid as honey.

"I would rather go hungry and walk around in rags than see you completely disregard Henry-James's pain!" Kady cried.

"You would rather see me disregard the code I live by, is that it?" Uncle Drayton said.

"Well, really, Daddy, you're disregarding that already."

Austin felt his eyes popping. That had come from Polly, who stepped forward, smoothing her skirt with her hands.

"You, too?" Uncle Drayton said to her. "I've come to expect your sister to contradict everything I say, but not you."

"Now, Daddy, just listen," Polly said. Her voice was soft and calm. "You're disobeying your own rules. Henry-James was just now brought in by the Patty Rollers, and you've already told him to go find a barrel so you can whip him." She folded her hands demurely at her waist. "I have always heard you say that you will never whip a slave without following the proper procedure."

What procedure? Austin thought. *Why is she reminding him? Hush up, Polly!*

Polly began to count off on her fingers. "One, you wait 24 hours before the whipping so it isn't done in the heat of the moment. Two, you never whip unfairly or for something small. Three, no slave gets more than 15 lashes. And four, you tell the slave why he's being punished."

"Don't forget the rest of the rules, Polly," Kady said angrily. "Use a cat-o'-nine-tails as broad as your hand from thumb to little finger and cut it into strips so it will hurt more. Oh, and make the whole whipping a big ritual so you can show that *you* are the king and they are mere nothings."

"Daddy isn't like that," Polly said. Her voice was still serene, but she was looking at Kady with dagger eyes that said, *Hush up, I know what I'm doing.*

I wish you'd *hush up, Polly,* Austin thought. *You're making this worse.*

"You want to be fair, don't you?" Polly said to her father. "Wait 24 hours."

"All right!" Uncle Drayton said impatiently. "Go on, boy! Go wash your face and lay my fire. I want my boots polished and my clothes laid out. I'm going to the church to vote tomorrow."

He stormed into the library and slammed the door behind him. Henry-James bolted out the front door, hands still tied behind his back, and Aunt Olivia and Mousie returned to the dining room, Mousie patting her mistress's brow all the way.

As soon as the dining room door closed, Kady jabbed her hands onto her hips. "Thank you very much, Polly!" she said, with venom in her voice. "I was beginning to think you'd changed, but I can see you are just as much of a little pet as you ever were. I was trying to help Henry-James—"

"And I *did* help him," Polly said. To Austin's surprise, she was still as calm as bathwater. "You have 24 hours, don't you?" She looked up at Austin at the banister. "You can do a lot in 24 hours, Boston Austin. I would get to work if I were you."

✛ ❖ ✛

Chapter Ten

Sally Hutchinson clapped her thin hands. "Polly, you are a smart girl."

"Smarter than I gave you credit for," Austin said. "Who would have thought you'd come up with that?"

"I'd stop while I was ahead if I were you, Austin," his mother said.

Polly waved that off with a lilting laugh and a waft of her hand. "I just feel that a man wants a wife who can calm him down when he's upset and show him the sensible thing to do without making him look the fool in front of others." She smiled at them all. "I was just practicing."

There was a unanimous groan. But as Polly passed him going up the stairs, Austin thought about it again: Polly just looked different these days. Her hair looked more like sausages than macaroni, and she was—

He was going to think "almost pretty," but he pushed that aside. Nah, Polly was still Polly. He just didn't feel like kicking her all the time anymore.

As his mother went by, he caught her hand. "I want to go back out to the cabin and see about Bogie," he said. "Can I, please?"

"You *may*," she said. "And then you need to rush right back.

101

We have some things to talk about."

Austin grinned. They did have plans to make if they were going to save Henry-James from a whipping tomorrow.

He and Charlotte both went to the cabin. Bogie was still lying with his eyes closed. He wasn't bleeding anymore, and there were no more groans from the pit of his soul. But Ria shook her head when Austin proclaimed him healed.

"He far from that, Massa Austin," she said. "Till he sit up and bark, ain't no tellin' what's gonna happen."

"Are you praying, Daddy Elias?" Austin said.

" 'Course I am."

"Did Henry-James find whoever shot Bogie?" Charlotte said.

"No," Ria said. "Only thing brightened his face when he come in here to wash up was the sight of that dog still breathin'.'"

"I'm praying that we can find out—and whoever it is is going to be sorry."

"Mmmm-mmmm-mmmm," Daddy Elias said. "And you gonna throw the first stone, Massa Austin?"

"I hope so," Austin said. "Henry-James should really do it, but they'd never let him."

"Mmmm-mmmm-mmmm," Daddy Elias said again.

When Austin crept into his mother's room, she was sitting by the fire, watching the flames but, he knew, not seeing them. Her eyes were far away, and his father's picture was on the table near her hand.

"You're thinking about Father," Austin said.

"I am."

Austin flopped down into another of Aunt Olivia's brocade chairs—hoping secretly that he was leaving some slave cabin dirt on it—and folded his arms over his chest. "I think about him a lot, too, especially when Uncle Drayton is being so ugly. Of course, right now, I have so many other things to think about.

Bogie, our plan for tomorrow. . . . Do you have any ideas—you know, about how we can change Uncle Drayton's mind about the whipping?"

Mother pulled her eyes from the fire and shook her head at him. "The only ideas I have are about how to get in touch with your father and get him here."

"By tomorrow?" Austin said. He felt his face scrunching up. "I don't think Uncle Drayton would listen to him anyway. He never does."

"Not to prevent a whipping, my love," she said. "To take us back north with him."

Austin was sure his heart stopped beating. "You mean, leave Canaan Grove right now?"

Mother nodded. "I'm well enough. And I don't know how much longer I can stand by and watch what's happening here. Kady being treated like a piece of property, Henry-James worse. Every time I think Drayton is coming around he does something beastly." She looked firmly at Austin. "You will *not* witness that whipping tomorrow night."

"But there isn't going to *be* a whipping! If we all put our heads together, we'll figure something out. We always do."

"My love, there might not be a whipping, but that isn't the whole of it. You can't change Uncle Drayton. I thought there was hope for him. We talked so much in Flat Rock last summer, and I know he has a good head on him, the way he refuses to go along with secession. But your father and I have learned in all our work that the way of slavery and what it gives people is sometimes so deep in them, they aren't ever going to change. I think Uncle Drayton is one of those people." She brushed a wisp of her doe-colored hair off her forehead. "I'm sorry, Austin."

"You go," Austin said. He could hear his voice teetering. "Take Jefferson, and I'll stay. I'll be all right."

"I know you love it here with your friends, but believe me, it's going to be so much worse if you have to watch Henry-James suffer, the way I had to watch Ria."

"But I want to be here with him! I can help!"

"I don't see what you could do, my love."

"I can do a lot. I've got Jesus on my side, like Daddy Elias says. Don't you even believe that?"

"I believe Jesus helps us accomplish what's possible."

"But this isn't impossible. I know it! Don't make me go!"

"I have to."

Austin's thoughts thrashed around. "But this isn't fair! It's just like Uncle Drayton telling Kady she has to get married. You think *he's* wrong."

"This is not quite the same thing."

"Yes, it is! You're being a hypocrite!"

"Austin, *enough*."

It was the sharpest tone she had ever used with him, and it stopped him in the middle of his next word. He gnawed miserably at his lip.

"Can I—*may* I go now?" he said.

"Please do," she said. "Before we say more things we'll be sorry for."

Austin was sure he wasn't sorry for anything he'd said. But he was also sure he'd never spent a more miserable night.

He flopped like a flounder in the bed next to Jefferson, but sleep never came. When the night turned to a gray morning mist, he was still staring at the ceiling, still worrying about Bogie, still torn in half between Canaan Grove and his father, and still as far away as ever from a plan to keep Henry-James from going over that barrel.

The face that looked back at him from the looking glass over the basin and pitcher as he washed was baggy-eyed and pale. Charlotte noticed it first thing at the breakfast table. Kady wasn't there, and Charlotte slipped into her seat across from Austin.

"Are you sick?" she said.

Austin shook his head miserably. It would be as hard to leave Lottie as it would Henry-James. What if they tried to marry *her* off? What if she couldn't stand up to Aunt Olivia and Uncle Drayton and the rest of them all by herself?

What if he never found another friend like her who liked plans and adventures and pretending, and who could almost read his thoughts?

He stared down at the eggs and sausages, potatoes and buckwheat pancakes, and he put his fork down. Suddenly, he just wasn't hungry anymore.

"Please pass the preserves," Aunt Olivia said crisply.

"Where's Daddy?" Polly said.

"He's already gone to the church to vote. He said there was sure to be a line. Every man in the parish is expected to vote in an election as important as this one."

"Kady thinks every woman should be allowed to vote, too," Polly said. She poured herself a cup of tea and cocked her head at Austin. "Tea?"

Austin shook his head. She was playing wife again. He wasn't in the mood.

"What do you think, Austin?" she went on. "Do you think women should be allowed to vote?"

Austin was saved from that conversation by the opening of the door. Uncle Drayton looked breathless and windblown. Henry-James was behind him carrying his master's discarded coat.

"How quickly can we get packed, Livvy?" he said.

"To go where?" she said.

"Charleston. It's nine o'clock in the morning and all of St. Paul's Parish has already voted. I want to be in Charleston when the results come in. This could change our lives, Olivia."

"Who is going?" Aunt Olivia said. Her double chins were quivering.

"All of us, and we'll need Mousie and Henry-James. We may have to stay a few days."

"And Tot?" Polly said.

"Of course. Go and get your things together."

Austin didn't move. No one had said whether the Hutchinsons would be going along. Somehow, he rather doubted it. And what if Father came while everyone was gone and took them back north?

"Go, Austin," Uncle Drayton said. "And tell you mother it's colder on the water in Charleston. She'll need warm clothes."

Aunt Olivia sniffed. When she wasn't looking, Charlotte silently clapped her hands.

"What about Bogie, though?" Austin whispered to her as they hurried out of the dining room.

"Ask your mother if Ria can stay here with him," she whispered back.

"I know one thing for sure," Polly put in as she and Tot swept past them. "It looks like there will be no whipping today."

She tossed her curls smugly and rustled off toward the stairs. Austin grinned so hard it hurt. Who said Jesus didn't help with the impossible?

The boat ride to Charleston was, as Austin put it in his mind, "amazing." The air was bracing, but the sun was warm on their faces as Charlotte, Austin, Henry-James, Kady, and Jefferson stood on the deck and watched the Ashley River go by. Polly looked torn but finally decided to sit in the ladies' cabin with Mother and Aunt Olivia.

"More wife practice," Austin muttered.

"Look at that," Kady said. She pointed to the reflection of the autumn trees on top of the water. "They just sizzle, don't they?"

"Looks like needlepoint to me," Austin said.

"I'm telling you, you're a poet," Kady said.

Austin shook his head. "Not me. I'm a scientist. Now that tree—"

"We know," Charlotte said. "Liveus oakus or something."

"*Taxodium distichium*," Austin said.

He spent the rest of the afternoon naming for them the little turtles sunning themselves on logs and the bulrushes poking up on the sides of the river. Henry-James pointed out what good soup turtles made, and Jefferson wished they would see an alligator or two. Kady drifted away and wrote furiously in her notebook.

But at least there were no fights, no threats, no reminders of scary, ugly things. Uncle Drayton stayed below deck for the three hours it took to get to Charleston.

And then the excitement of being there took over everything.

Charleston was a peninsula that pushed like an arrowhead from between the Ashley and the Cooper Rivers into the Atlantic Ocean. The harbor on the Ashley River side was alive with plantation flats, sloops and small schooners bobbing in and hugging the wharves, and gentlemen and ladies hurrying from the docks in their silk top hats and ostrich plumes. There were fewer loads of cotton and rice today than citizens of South Carolina bustling toward Meeting Street to hear the news.

"Have they declared a winner yet?" Uncle Drayton called to a man in a gray topper as the Ravenal boat pulled into the slip.

"Not yet," the man called back.

Austin cared less about who won the election than he did about seeing Charleston again. He'd only been here twice, once when he and his family had arrived on the train last winter, only to be swept off at once to Canaan Grove, and once in the spring. That had been an unhappy visit with nearly disastrous results.

"Remember the last time we were here?" Charlotte whispered to him as they climbed into one of the two carriages that were waiting there for them.

"I'm trying not to," Austin whispered back. But what he did like remembering as he kept his face pressed to the carriage window was the way Charleston looked with its colonial tile roofs, its quaint narrow alleys, its cobblestone streets.

"It's such a charming city," Sally Hutchinson said.

Aunt Olivia sniffed, for the fiftieth time since they'd started out. "It's elegant is what it is."

Uncle Drayton laughed—a sad laugh, Austin thought. "The Charlestonian is convinced that South Carolina is the best state in the Union, that Charleston is the greatest city in South Carolina, and his own family is the best family in Charleston."

"You've changed your mind about some of that, haven't you?" Mother said.

Uncle Drayton's face darkened. "I'll tell you after I hear the election results," he said. "I want to see how my fellow Charlestonians react."

And this time there was no laugh, sad or otherwise.

But Austin wasn't ready to be stifled yet. Charleston was too exciting.

He pointed at the green light poles that lined the streets. "Did you know that Charleston was one of the first cities in America to use gas lights? They've been here since 1848—a year before I was even born!"

"We're not backward, you know," Aunt Olivia said, with the inevitable sniff.

They were headed toward the East Battery, which Austin had read was set up in the 1750s to defend the city. He also knew that was where the Ravenals had their townhouse, where they stayed in the winter during the social season. He'd never seen it, but he'd heard Polly and Olivia go on practically for hours talking about how fine the homes were.

It took them a while to get there. Everyone in Charleston and the surrounding areas seemed to be in town. Carefully groomed horses pulling polished carriages were tangled with wagons and carts and omnibuses, clogging Meeting Street as they traveled south. Anticipation seemed to quiver out of every vehicle as everybody from well-dressed ladies with parasols to poor whites in overalls shouted about the election.

"What are those ornaments people are wearing on their jackets?" Polly said as she craned her neck around Austin to see.

"If it's the latest fashion, I know you'll have one before the day's over," Kady said.

"Can you find out, Drayton?" Aunt Olivia said.

Charlotte rolled her eyes at Austin. He could feel a twinkle coming into his. He leaned his body down past his shoulders out the window.

"Hey, mister!" he called out to a man who was weaving his way on foot through the traffic jam. "What's that thing on your lapel?"

The man looked down at the cockade of palmetto leaves he had pinned to his coat. "It's the symbol for Southern Independence!" he called back. "You'd better get yourself one if you want to stay in Charleston!"

Austin pulled his head in and looked at Uncle Drayton.

"Never mind," his uncle said. "I heard."

"I suppose I won't be getting one of those," Polly muttered. And the carriage fell silent.

They finally emerged from the knot of barouches and broughams and began to pass the grand houses Austin had heard about. He rode with his mouth continually dropped open.

He'd always thought the mansion at Canaan Grove was the fanciest home he'd ever seen, but these made that look like Henry-James's slave cabin. All of them were three and four stories tall with wide, rounded piazzas, big enough for even Polly's hoop skirts. Some had steps coming up to either side of the front porch with curlicued wrought iron railings and even fancy boot scrapers at the bottom of the steps.

Most of the houses were painted pastel colors—pale salmon pink, soft buttery yellow.

"They must paint them pale so they'll shed the heat," Austin said. "What color is yours?"

He got his answer as they turned left at the end of Meeting Street and onto the East Battery. The carriages stopped in front of a three-story brick building with Corinthian columns that rivaled the Greeks and a parapet across the front where an elaborate Ravenal family coat of arms was displayed. Every one of the over 20 windows Austin could see was framed in shining black shutters, and each of the ones on the side had an iron balcony. Austin began at once to weave stories for the games they could play on those.

"So this is your home away from home," Mother said as she stepped out of the carriage.

"It may not be for long," Uncle Drayton said. "We'll see."

And with tight lips he unlocked the garden gate and led them inside.

Charlotte began to show Austin and Jefferson around. But they saw only the big bay-shaped rooms on the south that overlooked the maze of formal gardens, the grand swirling staircase, and the ballroom with its glittering chandelier before Aunt Olivia ordered them to dress for dinner. There was a table reserved for them at the Mills House Hotel.

"I'd rather stay here and explore," Austin told his mother as he stood wearing his dark blue suit while she adjusted his tie.

"I know," she said. "But Uncle Drayton needs our support when the new President is announced. He may not have it much longer."

Austin frowned. "You mean, because you're mad at him?"

"No, because we may be leaving." She gave his short waistcoat-vest a tug. "But please, let's not argue about that to-night. Have a wonderful time—the Mills House is quite something."

As it turned out, the whole night was "quite something." By the time everyone was dressed and back in the carriages, it was growing dark, but the streets were blazing like sunshine itself with the gas lamps and the torches that lined them. Austin sat up front with Henry-James and the hired driver who was gnawing at his lower lip as he navigated the carriage through the throng of cheering people.

"I ain't never seen so many buckra at one time," Henry-James said.

"What's a *buckra?*" Austin said.

"That's a white man all gussied up to beat all." Henry-James showed his tooth-gap in a grin. "Kinda like you tonight, Massa Austin."

Austin curled his lip. "I hate getting dressed up."

Henry-James wriggled inside his blue plush uniform. "Onliest thing I likes 'bout it is I's warm for a change."

Dinner at the Mills House was outrageously elegant. That's how Austin thought of it as shiny-faced black servers with miles of gold braid brought tray upon tray of curried oysters, shrimp gumbo, she-crab soup, fricasseed scallops, and roast quail.

"Don't eat too much," Polly whispered to him. "You'll want to save room for the Huguenot torte. It's divine."

Austin was about to ask what a Huguenot torte was when a murmur traveled down the table. He looked up to see the source of it. Very-blond Garrison McCloud was standing at the head next to Uncle Drayton.

"There you are!" Uncle Drayton said as he stood up to take his hand. "I was beginning to think you'd decided not to come."

"He would never do anything of the kind," Aunt Olivia oozed.

"A gentleman never stands a lady up."

"They invited him here?" Charlotte whispered fiercely in Austin's ear. "Look at Kady. I've never seen her so mad."

Austin hadn't either. Kady's face was the color of the strawberry preserves, and she was clenching her white linen napkin until her knuckles matched it. Garrison didn't seem to notice. He slid into the chair next to her like a crown prince and dazzled a practiced smile up and down the table. Polly dazzled one back.

"I apologize for my tardiness," Garrison said. "I had important business at the Citadel."

"Is it secret?" Uncle Drayton said. "I know how these military matters are."

Garrison looked cautiously over both shoulders and leaned in. Polly and Aunt Olivia leaned in with him.

"It's fairly certain from the earliest telegrams that Abraham Lincoln will be elected. That means the South will surely secede." He put a reassuring hand on Kady's arm—which she stared at with her lip curled. "I know how you and your daddy feel about secession, but we must be prepared nevertheless. Several Federal military officials are resigning their posts even now, ready to serve the new southern nation. I'm considering doing the same myself."

Kady yanked her arm away. "Which is precisely why you and I could never—"

"Ladies and gentlemen of Charleston!" a deep male voice suddenly cried out above the chattering diners. "I have news!"

All talking stopped, and all clinking forks stilled. Necks strained toward the man in the doorway to the dining room.

"It is all but official!" he cried. "Abraham Lincoln has been elected President of the United States!"

✛ ✛ ✛

Chapter Eleven

There was a stunned silence in the dining room. The only person Austin expected to cheer was his mother, although she only closed her eyes as if she were praying. But to Austin's surprise, one man shot up from his chair and waved his bowler hat above his head.

"Ladies and gentlemen!" he shouted. "The South is going to rise. It's going to rise tonight!"

The Mills House was suddenly alive with shouts and whoops as if a war had already been fought and won—and every Yankee had been put properly in his place. People left their quail and oysters untouched and dashed out into the street, where Austin could hear music blaring.

Garrison McCloud scraped back his chair and held out his hand to Kady. "Come on, Miss Kady," he said. "We don't want to miss the celebration."

She looked at his hand for a long moment.

She wants the slaves free, but she doesn't want a war, Austin thought. *Wonder what she'll do.*

There was certainly no doubt in Polly's mind. She put her gloved hand up to Garrison with a delicate wave. "I wouldn't miss the celebration for the world," she said.

113

"All right then, Miss Polly," Garrison said. He held out an arm to her. "I hear there's going to be cannon fire and everything."

Austin was pretty interested in that himself. He went for the door with Charlotte, Kady, and Jefferson right behind him. He hoisted Jefferson up onto his shoulders when they got outside, so he could see the parade of Southrons passing on the street, carrying flags and waving banners.

"Where's the parade headed?" Garrison called out to them.

"Bonfire on the Battery!" a man with seven palmetto cockades on his hat brim shouted back.

The Ravenals and Hutchinsons all followed, the children scuttling curiously back and forth through the mass of people, the adults trudging behind with concerned looks. Uncle Drayton suddenly seemed 10 years older to Austin than he had this morning.

Garrison was right—a celebration cannon did fire into the air from the Battery, and the crowd cheered and hugged each other. Austin pushed back his sleeves and looked down at his arms. The excitement was so sharp that it had put goose bumps on his skin.

The crowd shushed itself as a distinguished-looking gentleman was helped up onto a platform. It was hard for Austin to see him, but he heard Kady whisper, "That's William Rhett."

"Is he related to Virgil?" Austin whispered back.

Kady nodded. "They're cousins. I've heard William has a lot more sense than Virgil. We'll see what he has to say."

"Abraham Lincoln has been elected!" William Rhett shouted. "And if you don't know what that means to South Carolina, I'm here to tell you."

There was a cheer as if he already had. On Austin's shoulders, Jefferson cheered right along with them.

William Rhett hushed them with his hands. "It means the tea has been thrown overboard. The revolution of 1860 has been initiated!"

A roar went up from the crowd. Torches, flags, and banners

waved, and hats and gloves were tossed until the air was thick with them.

"What tea?" Jefferson shouted down into Austin's ear.

Austin was pretty sure William Rhett was talking about the tea the colonists had thrown into the Boston Harbor back in the 1700s to protest the unfair government of the English king. If that was true, there really was going to be another war.

"Our first step!" Rhett shouted when he had the crowd settled down again. "Our first step is to hold a convention to vote on the question of secession."

"What question?" someone called up from the crowd. "There's no question in my mind!"

"Even so," William Rhett cried over the approving cheers, "we must discuss this like gentlemen and put it to a vote."

This time there was no silencing the cheering and hollering. Uncle Drayton gathered his group to him like a commanding mother hen.

"Back to the house," he said, his face solemn and dark. "It's too dangerous out here for us right now."

"But Daddy!" Polly said, pulling her mouth into a pout. "I'll be safe out here with Garrison."

"Your daddy is right," Garrison McCloud said quickly. "I would hate to see anything happen to you."

That seemed to be the second best answer Polly could have gotten. She smiled up at him coyly. Behind her back, Charlotte pretended to throw up.

"I wish we could stay out," Austin whispered to her. "Do you think your father would let us if we had Henry-James with us?"

They didn't even have a chance to ask. They hadn't moved two steps toward the east side of the park when two men planted themselves in front of the group. Tall, tangle-browed Virgil Rhett folded his arms and cocked his head back.

"Where are you running off to, Mr. Ravenal?" he said.

"Home with my family," said Uncle Drayton. "We have nothing to celebrate."

"Not even your Yankee relatives?" Chesnut put in. He was wheezing already and plucking at his bearlike side whiskers.

"Excuse me, gentlemen," Uncle Drayton said. "We'd like to be on our way."

Virgil Rhett put his hand on Uncle Drayton's chest to stop him. "Not until you tell us which side you stand on, Ravenal!"

"You know where I stand. I've made that plain enough."

"We just thought you might have come to your senses," said Chesnut. "Now that you see which way the wind is blowing."

"The wind hasn't changed as far as I'm concerned. Our convention will decide that."

Chesnut drew in a wheezy breath and flared his wide nostrils. "*Our* convention?" he said. "If you are not with us, how do you figure you have anything to do with this decision?"

"Because there are two sides to the question!" Uncle Drayton said. Austin could tell he was barely keeping himself from shouting. Charlotte moved closer to him. Behind Uncle Drayton, Henry-James was flexing and relaxing his fists and swallowing hard.

"The side of reason should be heard," Uncle Drayton went on. "And I intend to be there and speak for it."

"Over my dead body!" Chesnut said, his thick face reddening. "You're not welcome, Ravenal!"

"I don't need to be welcome. But you can count on my being there."

"And you can count on trouble," Virgil Rhett said.

"It can't be any worse than what you've brought on me already."

Virgil Rhett gave a hard laugh. "Oh, yes, it can, Ravenal. Oh, yes, it can."

Sally Hutchinson put an arm around each of her boys and

steered them off toward the East Battery. Behind them, Virgil Rhett's harsh laughter tangled up with the shouting and the music and the cannon fire and was lost in it.

"Olivia, do not unpack," Uncle Drayton said as he marched his brood up to the brick mansion. "I am taking all of you back to Canaan Grove first thing in the morning."

Polly started to wail, but Uncle Drayton cut her off with a look.

Austin himself was secretly glad. He wanted to get back to Bogie and Daddy Elias and the plantation itself, where you could find places to get away from shouting and threats and trouble.

He didn't know how wrong he was.

They arrived at Canaan Grove before noon, and Josephine hustled to get a cold dinner on the table. No one ate it anyway—because the first words out of Uncle Drayton's mouth when they sat down were, "Kady, I have made up my mind. You will marry Garrison McCloud as soon as your mother can put a wedding together."

"Drayton, that will take months!" Aunt Olivia cried.

"I want it done before secession is declared, which could be as soon as December."

"What about what *I* want?" Kady cried. She shoved her chair back and leaned across the table at her father. "Don't I have any say in this at all?"

"I wish I could give you some, Kadydid," Uncle Drayton said. He looked as if he were trying to smile. "But I have no choice either. I must make decisions and I must make them quickly, for the welfare of this family. I want you taken care of before everything goes up in smoke."

"What about me?" Polly said. "I *want* to marry Garrison McCloud!"

"I'll have to take my chances with you, Pumpkin Polly," Uncle

Drayton said. "You're too young to marry. It would be like selling you off into slavery."

"Oh, but it isn't where I am concerned!" Kady said. She threw her dark curls over her shoulder and snatched up her skirts.

"Where are you going?" Aunt Olivia said. "We have a wedding to plan!"

"Go ahead and plan it, Mama," Kady said. "You've planned the rest of my life without me, so why not this?"

She bolted from the table, and the preserved cucumbers and the pickled peaches sloshed their juice out of their bowls. Mousie hurried to dab at the tablecloth with a napkin, and Aunt Olivia brushed her away.

"Drayton, when did our Kady become such an ungrateful child?" she said, chins vibrating madly.

"When she stopped having anything to be grateful for, I would imagine," said Sally Hutchinson. "If you'll excuse me?"

Austin was sure he heard tears at the edge of her voice as she hurried from the room.

We'll be leaving for sure now, Austin thought miserably. He looked at Charlotte, whose tears were welling up in her eyes. She got up without excusing herself and ran out, too.

In his corner behind Uncle Drayton, Henry-James followed her out with his eyes. But his body stayed stiff even after he winced at the slamming of the door. Austin stared at him until he got his black friend to look at him.

Do you want me to go after her for you? Austin said with his eyes.

Henry-James gave the biggest nod he could risk.

Austin tossed his napkin on the table and made for the door.

"What has happened to manners in this house?" he heard Aunt Olivia say.

Charlotte was almost to Rice Mill Pond when Austin caught up to her. The air had turned November cold, and it was drying his hands and biting at his throat as he fell into running-step beside her. Without a word to him, Charlotte clawed her way up an oak and clung to one of its branches high up. Austin had to settle for the one just below hers and catch his breath before he could talk.

"You're mad about Kady," he said finally.

"She can't leave!" Her voice caught like it had been snagged on a hook.

"Don't you remember my mother saying Uncle Drayton smolders in his ashes or something? He'll probably change his mind—"

"No, he won't. You don't know, Austin!"

"But he's changed his mind about a lot of things." He put up his fingers to start counting them off, but Charlotte shook her head so hard that a half dozen leaves sailed toward the ground.

"He has that look on his face. I saw it there one other time, and that time he didn't change his mind, no matter what."

"When was that?" Austin said.

"When he decided to let you and Aunt Sally and Jefferson come here and live with us. Mama didn't like it."

"I know," Austin said matter-of-factly. "She hates us. That's because she's a hypocrite."

"Daddy wasn't. He said he loved his sister and there was nothing he wouldn't do for her when she needed him and that was that." Charlotte put a hand up to her eyes. "Why can't he do that with Kady? Why is he making her go away with that boy she doesn't even like?"

"Because he's a hypocrite, too," Austin said. He was getting gladder by the minute that he'd learned that word. "But we're not, and we can do something about this."

Charlotte shook her head again. "I don't think so, Austin. Not this time."

"But this isn't right," Austin said stubbornly, "and we have to do what's right, even if your father doesn't. Otherwise, we're as bad as him."

Charlotte watched her feet swing. Her bottom lip was quivering. "I don't know—I'm scared."

"You've been scared plenty of times, but you always go right ahead with the plan. Remember that time—?"

"What plan?" she said.

Austin gave a sheepish shrug. "I don't know yet. But we'll think of something. And one thing is for sure."

"What?"

"Your daddy has forgotten about whipping Henry-James. He has too many other things to think about."

That made her smile from one corner of her mouth. "So are you thinking of something?" she said.

"Always," Austin said. "Now, come on, while we're thinking, we can go see Bogie."

Charlotte nodded eagerly, and they both scrambled down from the tree. Just as they hit the ground, Austin heard a door slam, and he looked back toward the spring house. A figure clad in a dark cape was hurrying away from it, carrying a lumpy bag over one shoulder. Something dropped from it as the figure hurried toward the bridge. The drying autumn wind swirled leaves around the slim person's feet and with a sharp snap flipped the hood back.

"Kady!" Charlotte said in a whisper.

"I thought she taught the slaves in there in the afternoons," Austin said. "I wonder why she's leaving?"

"What's that she has with her? Books, do you think? I thought I saw one drop."

Austin strained to see, but Kady was already disappearing into the bushes at the bank of the pond. She reappeared crossing the bridge, her cape flying out behind her.

"That's an old cape of Mama's she had stored away in a trunk,"

Charlotte said. "She was going to give it to Ria or somebody."

Austin watched Kady lose herself in the forest of cypress and sweet gum.

"Should we follow her?" he said.

Charlotte shook her head. "You know how she likes to go off by herself and write in her notebook."

"At a time like this?" Austin said.

"Maybe she's writing a poem about it," Charlotte said.

"Huh," Austin said. " 'Daddy says I must marry that red-faced man . . . so I'm running away as fast as I can.' "

Charlotte stared at him blankly. "That was stupid, Austin."

Austin grinned. "It was the best I could do. I told you, I'm a scientist, not a poet."

"So put your scientist mind to work and think of a way to save her," Charlotte said.

"Let's at least go see what she dropped."

They both headed toward the bridge. Nimble Charlotte got there first and picked up the dropped object. She was brushing it off when Austin reached her side.

"I guess she won't be writing a poem after all," Charlotte said. "It's her notebook."

"Miz Charlotte?" a tiny voice said. Mousie was creeping toward them, fretting with her little paws. "Missus say come on up to the Big House and have yourself measured for your dress for Miz Kady's weddin'."

"Already?" Austin said.

"Weddin' gonna be nex' week," Mousie said. "Missus 'bout to lose her mind."

Charlotte looked at Austin, eyes panicked.

"I'm thinking," Austin said. "I'm thinking really hard."

But think as he might, nothing came to him. It was hard to be inventive with the tension in the house so thick you could hack at it with a hatchet, and Aunt Olivia shrilling out orders to everyone.

"Josephine, check to see how much beef we have!"

"Mousie, where are my ink pens? I have to start writing invitations!"

"Polly, bring me those pictures of wedding gowns you have— the ones those French princesses wore!"

"Tot, bang on Kady's door one more time and tell her I'm making these plans without her!"

And even that wasn't as bad as the news Sally Hutchinson had for him. Austin wandered into her room just before supper, while Charlotte was being coerced into helping polish the silver downstairs. His mother looked up from the desk by the window and dipped her pen in the inkwell. She nodded to Ria, who got up and left.

Austin's heart turned over. "What's the matter? Is it Bogie?"

"No, my love," Mother said. "Bogie's the same."

Austin folded his arms uncomfortably across his chest. "Then why do you look like you wish I hadn't come in just now?"

"You're too smart for me," she said. She smiled faintly and pried out one of his hands. Reluctantly, he sat down. She was scaring him.

"What's wrong?" he said.

"You know yourself," she said. "Your uncle's gone crazy with this marriage of Kady's, the whole South has gone even crazier—"

"We're leaving, aren't we?" Austin said. "You were writing a letter to Father."

She pulled the smile firm and nodded. "Just as I said, you're too smart for me." She curled her fingers around his arm. "Now before you start hurling insults at me again, just listen. I've told your father we'll stay until he can see his way clear to come for us. Between talk of secession and your uncle's attitude, I think our time has come."

Austin's throat got tight. He glared down at the toes of his ankle jackboots. "I don't see how this is any different from Uncle Drayton telling Kady she has to marry Garrison McCloud. He says he's doing it to protect her—and that's what you're saying."

"I'm trying to protect you from being hurt, possibly killed," Mother said. "Uncle Drayton is protecting Kady from being poor and a social outsider. There's a difference. Kady would survive, but you might not."

"Who's going to get killed?" Austin said. "Not me!"

"Don't tell me, Austin, that you haven't already figured out that we're the enemy here in the South. We're the very ones people are going to shoot at if a war starts." She pressed her hands to her temples. "And after what I saw last night, I think that's exactly what's going to happen."

"But there's too much to do now!"

She patted his leg. "I'm going to rest now. My head is pounding."

Austin didn't see anyone the rest of the evening. Aunt Olivia had Polly and Charlotte in the drawing room with the door closed, and she called out once for tea and bread and about a hundred times for pins and food lists and more ink for her inkwell. Uncle Drayton stayed in the library with his door locked. And after the fourth attempt, nobody even bothered knocking on Kady's door anymore. Austin played dominoes with Jefferson and put him to bed, and then lay awake staring at the ceiling.

"Jesus?" he whispered. "If I'm not a hypocrite and all these other people are, then why are they getting their way and I'm not? And Henry-James isn't, and Kady isn't?"

He didn't expect an answer, and he didn't get one. He stared up again until there was a tap on the door. Charlotte padded in and hurried to his bed. She was barefoot but still in her clothes, and her eyes were saucer-wide and glistening.

"Austin!" she whispered with tears in her voice. "Kady's run away!"

ustin sat straight up in bed. Beside him, Jefferson mumbled in his sleep, and Austin motioned Charlotte toward the window. In the cold light of the moon, her face was so pale that her freckles stood out in dark points.

"How do you know?" he hissed to her.

She held up a piece of paper. Austin clutched it in the moonlight and saw round, girlish writing hurriedly scrawled across it in pencil. It said:

Dearest Charlotte,
I've gone away. Don't worry about me. I couldn't leave without saying good-bye. I love you, sister.
Kady

"What if she's out in the woods somewhere?" Charlotte whispered frantically.

"And what's going to happen when your father finds out she's gone?" Austin shivered. "What if he finds her and brings her back—and then he punishes her and *still* makes her get married?"

"Austin!" Charlotte hissed. "You're not making me feel better!"

"Sorry," Austin said. He wasn't making himself feel much better either.

Suddenly, there was a shaft of light across the room. Both Charlotte and Austin jerked around to see Mother standing in the doorway with an oil lamp.

Charlotte thrust the note behind her back and looked guiltily up at Austin's mother. Austin groaned inside. Charlotte, he knew, would never make it as a spy.

"Oh, dear," Mother said. She moved softly toward them, holding the dull light out in front of her. "More secrets. By the looks on your faces, I think you'd better let me help you."

Charlotte didn't even give Austin a chance to stammer. She pulled out the note and stuck it straight at Mother. She took it and ran her eyes over it, then looked up at them sharply.

"We have to find her," she said. "Before her father does—before he even knows she's gone if we can. Do you have any idea where she might have gone?"

"We saw her this afternoon," Austin said. "She was leaving the spring house all wrapped in an old cape and carrying some kind of bundle, but we didn't even think she might be running off."

"Which way did she go?"

Charlotte and Austin looked fearfully at each other.

"Into the woods on the other side of Rice Mill Pond," Austin said.

Mother closed her eyes and shuddered. "All right," she said. "Kady was upset, but she's still too bright to just take off into the forest without a plan. Let's put our heads together now. Who does she know off in that direction?"

"The Singletons' plantation is down that way," Charlotte said. "But she wouldn't go there. They'd bring her right back to Daddy."

"Would she hide in the church, perhaps?" Mother asked. But

she shook her head. "The Reverend Pullens would never protect her. Drayton gives too much money to the church." She shook her head again. "I wish we could get our hands on that notebook of hers. She writes everything in there. That's the first thing she would put in that bag she was toting."

"She did," Charlotte said, "but it fell out."

Mother's eyebrows went up. "Do you have it?"

Charlotte nodded. "I'll go get it."

As she darted off, Mother squeezed Austin's hand. "I'm going to help you—and Kady—all I can," she said. "But if we don't find her before Uncle Drayton discovers she's gone, we have to tell him what you know. At least then he'll know she wasn't stolen away by the secessionists or something. He'll be frightened enough as it is."

"Good," Austin said.

"Now, Austin—"

But she was interrupted by Charlotte bursting through the doorway.

She pushed the door closed with her foot and leaped toward them with the notebook in hand.

Mother took the book from Charlotte, but she only ran her hand across the cover and looked at it sadly.

"Why don't you open it and look for clues?" Austin said.

"I just hate to peek into her private life," Mother said. "She has so little she can truly call her own." She sighed. "But it's to help her, I guess."

Charlotte nodded, and Austin nudged impatiently at the book. "Open it," he said.

Mother reverently pulled back the cover and turned the pages to the last few entries. She scanned the rounded handwriting, smiling slightly here, twisting her mouth a little there. Austin squirmed and stretched his neck to look between the pages.

"What's that drawing?" he said.

Mother leafed toward it and spread the pages open. It was a map, scratched out in pencil as if she had been in a hurry.

"I have no idea where this leads," she said. "Do you, Charlotte?"

Charlotte frowned over the page. "That's past the woods, up away from the river," she said. "I've never been that way. Mama never let us, so I forgot about it."

"Why wouldn't she let you?" Austin said. He could feel his ears perking up with interest.

"I don't know. She just said it wasn't a proper place for young ladies, and we had plenty of places to play right here on the plantation."

"Then why on earth would she have this?" Mother said.

"Read the poem next to it," Austin said. "She writes poems about everything."

Mother ran her finger down the page opposite the map, moving her lips as she silently read. At the bottom of the page she lifted her eyes, and her eyebrows, too.

"Listen to this," she said.

So many people say that they know what's best for Kady
They press her every day to become a southern lady
They bring the finest gentlemen their status can provide
With ruffled gowns and hair trims they shape the perfect bride
They say she has to sip her tea with Charleston's richest women
And swallow the rules of foolish men with brains like a persimmon
Funny how with all their wealth there's no one understands
But a gangly young'un with unschooled speech and field dirt on his hands
I tuck his map inside my book in case the night should come

When the only place where I am Kate is his bedraggled home.

"So that map leads to somebody's bedraggled home," Austin said.

"The only place where she can be herself," Mother said sadly. "I have a good mind to show this to Drayton right this minute."

"Please don't, Aunt Sally!" Charlotte said. "Daddy wouldn't understand!"

Mother nodded. "Just like the poem says." She closed the book and handed it to Charlotte. "It sounds like she had a place to go. And I don't think she eloped or anything foolish like that."

"What do we do now?" Austin said.

"I think we should sleep on it. If she doesn't come back on her own in the morning, perhaps someone can follow the map."

She kissed both their foreheads and left.

"I can't sleep on it, Austin," Charlotte said when she was gone. "I can't sleep at all—not with Kady off in some bedraggled house!"

"You're thinking what I'm thinking," Austin said.

"That we should go find her tonight?"

Austin nodded. "We could get some pine knots from Henry-James and light them for torches. All we have to do is follow the map. It doesn't look that hard." He glanced sideways at Charlotte. "Only, you're not really supposed to go there."

"Nothing is the way it's supposed to be anymore," Charlotte said. "I'm going to get my shoes. I'll meet you outside. We won't make as much noise if we go one by one."

Austin pulled on a wool shirt and suspendered trousers and carried his boots down the back stairs. There was no need to worry about noise. Aunt Olivia was still in the drawing room, ranting to Mousie.

"I don't know why I'm bothering with these invitations. We've been shunned by all of Charleston. There won't be a soul at the wedding but us and the darkies!"

"There isn't even going to be a wedding if *we* have anything to do with it!" Austin muttered to himself as he slipped out the back door. Charlotte appeared a moment later with the notebook tucked under her green cape.

"First stop, Slave Street!" Austin whispered to her.

There was a tiny fire flickering at the cabin, but only Henry-James was still awake. He sat up with a jerk from his place next to Bogie in front of the fireplace as Austin tapped on the door and let himself in.

"How is he?" Austin whispered.

"He still can't walk," Henry-James said. "I got to carry him out every time he has to go pee." He ran his eyes silkily over Charlotte and Austin. "You come all the way out here this time o' night to see 'bout Bogie?"

"Well, no," Austin said. He tumbled out Kady's story and their plan and ended breathlessly with, "Do you have two pine knots we can use for torches?"

Henry-James got to his feet. "You ain't gonna need no torches with me along."

"No, Henry-James!" Charlotte hissed hoarsely. "We're going off the plantation. What about the Patty Rollers?"

"What about the two o' you wanderin' around out there in them woods in the dark?"

"We have a map," Austin said.

"And you ain't got a lick o' sense." Henry-James shook his head firmly. "I's sorry, Massa Austin, but you ain't takin' Miz Lottie off'n this land without me."

There was no arguing with Henry-James when his eyes turned to stones like that. Those were the times Austin forgot Henry-James was a slave and could be ordered to do just about anything. And secretly, Austin was relieved that he was coming along.

They crept soundlessly from the cabin. The only noise was

Bogie whimpering to go along. It put a lump in Austin's throat.

"You'll be well enough before long, Bogie," Austin whispered to him.

Like three shadows, they slipped in and out of the poplars and sweet gum and down to the place where Rice Mill Pond turned into a stream. Once they jumped across and entered the inky blackness of the forest, Austin was in a place he'd never been before. He stayed right on Charlotte's heels—and she stayed on Henry-James's.

It was damp-cold, and a mist had formed on the forest floor. Austin's feet disappeared into it as they wove through the trees. Most of them had dropped their leaves, which made a slippery carpet on the ground. More than once Austin lost his balance and groped for the back of Charlotte's skirt. Every time he did, something would startle and skitter in the shadowy underbrush—and he could hear himself swallowing.

Austin was sure the sun would be coming up by the time they finally came out of the woods. But it was still eerie night as they emerged into a clearing and headed for some scattered trees, draped with witch-haired Spanish moss.

"Remember, it isn't even Spanish," Austin muttered to himself. It was reassuring to say something he knew for sure. The blackness was so unpredictable. He grunted. *And Charlotte and I were going to do this by ourselves!*

In the deeper shade of one large oak, Henry-James stopped and asked for the map. He squinted at it.

"How can you see?" Austin said. "I can barely see my hand!"

"Shhh!" Henry-James said. He looked out over the dusty clearing and pointed. "You see that there dog-trot house?"

"What's a dog-trot house?" Austin said.

"Ain't nothin' more'n a shack."

Austin peered through the mist and shadows and made out the outline of a shanty with a sagging roof and a porch that dipped like a washbasin. Its yard was strewn with mysterious shapes, which on inspection turned out to be wooden buckets, horse troughs, and discarded furniture. Henry-James's cabin was a mansion compared to this.

"What about it?" Austin whispered.

"That's what this here map is leadin' to," Henry-James said.

"Kady couldn't be here!" Charlotte whispered.

"But it's a 'bedraggled home'," Austin said. "Just like in the poem."

Charlotte gulped. "I guess there's nothing to do but go up to the door."

"You ain't doin' no such thing, Miz Lottie," Henry-James said. "Man lives there likely to greet you at the door with a rifle in his hand."

"Why?" Austin said.

" 'Cause we's beatin' on the door in the middle o' the night— and he got to guard what he got 'cause he ain't got much.'"

"I suppose it's up to me, then," Austin said.

He moved his feet, but he didn't go anywhere. Henry-James had a hand planted firmly on his shoulder.

"What you gonna do when you got a gun barrel up your nose, Massa Austin?" he said.

Austin shrugged his free shoulder. "I'll think of something. I always do."

"Words ain't no match for a flintlock rifle, Massa Austin. Now, I'm goin' to the door, and you two chilrun gonna stay right here under this tree till I finds out if'n Miz Kady even there." He stomped off toward the shack muttering, "Last thing I got to do is let them two get killed. I might as well be dead my own self."

Austin could barely stand to wait while Henry-James gingerly climbed the rickety steps to the dog-trot house. He probably would have followed him if Charlotte hadn't been wrapped around his arm like a baby possum. He held his breath and listened as Henry-James knocked—politely—on the door.

"I hope it doesn't fall off the hinges," Austin whispered.

It didn't, but it creaked as someone inside pushed it open. Austin stretched his neck to see if he could pick out the outline of a gun. He didn't see one.

He only saw a watermelon head on a skinny body.

harlotte gasped and slapped her hand over her mouth. Austin grabbed her by the wrist and took off toward the shanty. Narvel had taken enough menacing steps to bring him right into Henry-James's face when they got to the porch. Austin dropped Charlotte's hand and squeezed in between them.

"Well," Austin said, plastering a smile onto his face. "Fancy meeting you here!"

"This here's my house!" Narvel said through his tight teeth. "Where else would I be?"

"How would we know?" Austin said innocently. "You've never invited us over."

Narvel gave an ugly grunt. "That's right, I didn't. So what are you doing here?"

"Now you know, that's an intriguing thing," Austin said. He watched with satisfaction as a puzzled look came over Narvel's high-forehead face. Lots of big words. That should do it. "We've been looking for my cousin—Charlotte's sibling, Kady Ravenal. You may have made her acquaintance. Nonetheless, she seems to have absconded with herself, and we found among her belongings a map, which, for some unexplainable reason, led us straight here—to your humble abode."

Narvel blinked at Charlotte. "Is he speaking English?"

Charlotte gave a frozen nod. "Of course," she managed to say. "I understood every word." She nudged Henry-James with her elbow. "Didn't you, Henry-James?"

Henry-James bobbed his head respectfully and said, "Yes'm, Miz Lottie."

Austin gave Narvel an Uncle-Drayton-charming smile. "Imagine our surprise when we arrived and *you* opened the door. But I've recovered now and I'm wondering, may we speak to Miss Kady?"

"She ain't here!" Narvel said. He punctuated his sentence with a spit on the porch. "I don't know what you're talkin' about!"

Austin watched Narvel's spittle run into a crack in the board. This was the "gangly one with unschooled speech and field dirt on his hands"—who *understood?* Austin took a breath and managed another charming smile.

"She drew a map. You'll be flattered to know she even wrote a poem. She named this a 'bedraggled home.'"

Narvel inched his nose close to Austin's, so near that Austin could smell hog and hominy on his breath. "Bedraggled," Narvel growled. "What's that?"

Austin maneuvered himself away and waved a hand toward the yard. "It's a perfect description of your place," he said. "Ramshackle, disheveled, unkempt."

"Speak English!" Narvel shouted. With a snap too fast to see, he snatched up Austin's wrist and brought him up to his stormy green eyes.

"I am speaking English!" Austin shouted back. "You're just too stupid to understand! Maybe you'll get this—*where's Kady?*"

"I told you, I ain't seen her!"

"I'm here, Austin," said a voice from the doorway.

Three mouths fell open like trapdoors as Kady stepped out onto the porch with the black cape clutched around her. Narvel gave Austin's wrist a final, painful squeeze before he let go and moved protectively close to Kady. He frowned deep between his eyebrows as Charlotte shot past them all and flew into Kady's arms.

"How on earth did you find me here?" Kady said.

"You dropped your book," Charlotte said. "I'm sorry, but we looked through it and found the map and your poem." She pulled the notebook out of her cape and handed it to Kady, who hugged it to her chest.

"I thought I'd lost it," she said. "This will make the time go faster."

"Time till when?" Austin said. "Are you going to stay *here* forever? Why did you even end up here in the first place?"

Kady smiled a watery smile. "I was already missing all your questions . . . and all Jefferson's mischief . . . and all Polly's primping."

"Then come home," Charlotte said.

"Lottie, you know I can't. Mama probably has the wedding all planned by now, right?"

Charlotte nodded sadly. "Almost. I've already been measured for my dress."

"I still want to know why you're *here* of all places," Austin said. He glared at Narvel, who was glaring back and swallowing his Adam's apple up and down.

"Where else was I going to go, Austin? You remember that evening you found me crying? Narvel came across me, too, a little later. We got to talking and—"

"Wait," Austin said. "Narvel actually carried on a conversation?"

"*And*," Kady went on, widening her eyes sternly at Austin, "he said he knew just how I felt—supposedly free but still feeling like I was all locked up in a cage. He said if I ever did decide to run away for good, I could come here. He told me where he lived and I drew myself a map."

It was Austin's turn to widen his eyes. "You trusted a lying little cheater like him! I'm surprised he hasn't brought Uncle Drayton right to this door and asked for a reward for finding you!"

"I ain't done that, and I won't!" Narvel snapped. "Miss Kady don't treat us like the dirt on the bottom of her shoes, not like the rest of the Ravenals. She ain't never acted like she was better'n us—and I treat her the same—"

"What's goin' on out here?" someone growled.

The door was again pushed open, this time by a long object. It took Austin a moment to realize it was a rifle. It took Henry-James only a second, and he shoved Austin and Charlotte behind him and stood in front of them like a human shield.

"It's all right, Micah," Kady said. "It's my cousin and my sister. They were worried about me and came looking."

Micah slowly lowered the gun, but he kept a between-the-eyebrows scowl pointed at them. As he let out a breath, Austin noted that he was a shriveled-up version of Narvel—the piece of hair that hung over his too-high, wrinkled forehead was gray, his green eyes were the shade of stagnant pools, his mouth was so tight it looked as if it would have to be pried open.

"Get that darky off my porch," the man said. "I don't allow colored here."

"Micah—" Kady said.

But Henry-James shook his head. "No worry, Miz Kady," he said, eyes down. "I'll wait down here."

Micah watched him go, eyes glittering, and then shuffled back into his house. Austin could feel his backbone turning to barbed wire.

How can Kady stay in a house with people like this? his head was shouting at him.

"I am just going to stay here until I can think of what to do to keep from having to marry Garrison McCloud," Kady was saying. She rubbed the corners of her eyes. "Please don't tell Daddy I'm here. I just need time to think."

"He doesn't know you're gone yet," Charlotte said.

"But come tomorrow morning, Mama is going to start screaming. Please, you can't tell them where I am."

"If'n you do," Narvel said, "Mr. Ravenal will have my daddy's hide." He flipped back his stubborn sliver of hair. "Not that you care about that."

You're absolutely right, Austin almost said. But an idea snapped into place as if it had been waiting there all night.

"Do you promise?" Kady said.

"On one condition," Austin said.

Kady lifted her eyebrows at him. "What's that?"

Austin turned to the scowling Narvel. "None of us will tell Uncle Drayton that you're hiding Kady here if you'll promise to stop causing trouble for Henry-James."

Narvel's green eyes flashed only an instant of recognition before he flipped his stray strand of hair back and said, "That'll be easy. I ain't never done nothing to him in the first place."

"You are such a liar," Austin said. "But if you lie this time, you'll be in trouble—not from me, but from my uncle."

It was just then that the door squeaked open again. Austin expected to see Micah's hard mouth, but there was instead a row of six little faces squeezed into the opening, all with their black hair hanging in their too-hungry big eyes.

"Ya'll get back inside now!" Narvel barked at them.

"When we gonna eat, Narvel?" the tallest one asked. "The baby's hongry."

The one on the bottom popped his thumb into his mouth and begged Narvel with his eyes.

"I'm gonna go out and get us a squirrel just as soon's I'm through here. Ya'll git now, y'hear?"

They did as he said, the smallest one pulling his thumb out long enough to give Narvel a tiny-toothed smile.

Narvel waited until the door closed behind them before he looked back at Austin. "We need the work at Mr. Ravenal's," he said. "That's the only reason I'm promising. You don't tell, and I'll leave the darky alone."

"You can start by learning his name," Austin said. "He's not 'the darky'—he's Henry-James."

Narvel just nodded to Kady and flung himself into the house. A moment later, they heard the back door slam and footsteps crunch across the backyard.

"He's going to go hunt a squirrel at night?" Charlotte whispered to Austin.

But Austin had already erased Narvel from his mind. That was one problem taken care of, and he was feeling pretty smug about it.

"Well, thank you, Austin," Kady said. She looked a little dazed. "You know, I think there's something I need to do before you go back." She opened her notebook and pulled out the pencil she had stuck there. She sat down on the porch with a plop and began to scribble furiously.

"What are you doing?" Austin said.

"I'm writing a note to Mama and Daddy to let them know I'm safe. It's the least I can do for everybody."

"But if we give it to them, they'll know that we've seen you," Charlotte said. "They'll make us tell where you are!"

"Then we won't give it to them," Austin said. "We'll put it someplace where they'll find it." He could *feel* his eyes twinkling. "Let's see, where could we put it?"

"Here," Kady said, ripping the page out of the notebook and handing it to Charlotte. "Now, please go. It's getting late, and I don't want anyone to discover *you're* missing. And watch for the

Patty Rollers—the last thing we need is for Henry-James to get caught now."

"We're gone already," Austin said. He took the steps in one leap and looked over his shoulder at Kady. "Don't worry, you're on the winning side."

Charlotte gave Kady one last hug and they were off, running toward the woods with hearts like feathers. Even the shadows seemed lighter now. Austin laughed out loud as they charged into the trees.

"Kady's safe and so is Henry-James! Everything really *is* going to be all right!"

"That was your smartest idea yet," Charlotte said. "Now we don't have to worry about Narvel anymore."

"You done good, Massa Austin," said Henry-James. "If'n that boy keep his word, that is."

"I think he will," Austin said. He couldn't help puffing out his chest. "He doesn't dare make trouble for his father. I wouldn't either. That's one mean-faced man."

"Didn't you see those little children, though?" Charlotte said. "I think he did it for them."

"Narvel?" Austin said. He could feel his eyebrows wrinkling together. "Nah, he's too hateful."

"Stop!" Henry-James hissed.

He flung his black arm out, and both Charlotte and Austin plowed into it.

"What's wrong?" Austin said, bringing his voice down to a whisper.

"I heard somethin'. Quiet now."

Austin held his breath, and Charlotte edged closer to him. Henry-James stood, taut from head to foot. They listened until Austin was ready to tell him he'd been hearing things when a snap echoed through the woods.

"Somebody stepping on a stick," Charlotte mouthed to Austin.

There was a second snap. Henry-James grabbed Charlotte's hand and took off in the opposite direction. Heart throbbing in his throat, Austin followed at a skittering clip. Branches slapped his face and underbrush reached up to grab his calves, but he kept on. He had no idea what they were running from, but he did know Henry-James was bent on getting away from it, and fast.

They ran for what seemed like a mile, until Austin got an ache in his side.

"I think we've lost him, whoever he is," Austin said in a loud whisper.

"No, we ain't lost him," Henry-James flipped over his shoulder. "He just want us to think we did."

Even as Henry-James finished his sentence, Austin heard more twigs snapping behind them, as if their pursuer was tired of being careful. Henry-James let go of Charlotte's hand and pointed to a fallen tree.

"Crawl in there," he whispered.

"*In* there?" Austin whispered back.

But Henry-James pushed his head down and gave him a shove. The tree was hollow and long, and Charlotte had already squirmed her way into its dark insides. Austin wriggled in after her and felt Henry-James come in behind him.

He's facing out so he can see, Austin thought. *I wish I was. I can hardly breathe!*

Fear bolted through him, and he groped the side of the log. Something skittered under his palm.

"I have to get out!" he hissed. "Now!"

Henry-James nudged him hard with his foot, and Austin found his mouth with his hand and muffled a scream. Henry-James got stiff as a post, and Austin heard shuffling in the leaves.

"I'm tellin' you, they're gone. I doubt they was ever here to begin with," a voice growled.

It was Irvin Ullmann, the Patty Roller.

"And I'm tellin' *you* I seen the little cuffee!" another voice answered. Sniveling Barnabas Brown, of course.

"That darky would be even stupider than I took him for to leave Canaan Grove after we worked him over last time," Irvin said gruffly. "Now come on. It's too cold out here for me."

"Don't come cryin' to me when we ain't got enough money to feed ourselves this winter," Barnabas whined.

His voice trailed off through the forest. Henry-James didn't move until it disappeared completely. As soon as he did, Austin backed out like a skittish cat and sat on the ground, hugging his knees.

"Are you all right, Austin?" Charlotte said as she joined him, shaking the insects out of her cape.

"'Course he ain't," Henry-James said. "Don't nobody like bugs in they drawers—"

His voice was clipped off by a loud crack. It wasn't the snapping of a twig this time. It was a bang that cut through the night like a cracking whip.

Austin felt his skin go cold. "Was that a gun?"

"It's probably Narvel," Charlotte said. "Remember, he said he was going to go shoot a squirrel for the children's supper."

Henry-James's face hardened and his eyes narrowed. "If'n it was," he said, his voice as stony as his face, "then he's the one shot Bogie."

"You can tell by the shot?" Austin said. "Don't all guns sound alike?"

But Henry-James didn't answer. He had already taken off in the direction of the gun—and the Patty Rollers.

✛ ✛ ✛

Chapter Fourteen

"No!" Charlotte cried. And then she clapped both hands over her mouth. Her eyes were horrified.

"He's gonna get himself caught!" Austin hissed to her. And then another thought hit him. "And if he finds Narvel, we're all in trouble! Henry-James will jump him for sure, and Narvel will go back on his side of the deal."

"Come on," Charlotte said. Her hand was sweaty-cold on Austin's wrist. "We have to stop him!"

They tore off through the forest again, this time with no sure-footed Henry-James to follow. Austin put up his hand to shield his face. He felt a twig snag his wool shirt and he heard it rip, but he hurried on. Charlotte ran ahead of him, cape floating out behind her. When she came to a sudden halt, Austin stumbled over her and grabbed at a tree to catch himself. Charlotte shoved him behind it.

"What?" he whispered in her ear.

She pointed ahead. Two shadowy figures stood amid the trees, both twisting and turning as if they were looking for something.

"The Patty Rollers, I think," Charlotte whispered back.

"Do you see Henry-James?"

Charlotte shook her head and peeked out from behind the

tree. She snapped back, eyes popping. Austin looked where she pointed and felt his own eyes bulge.

Narvel Guthrie stood not four feet away, head cocked toward the sound he didn't yet know was the Patty Rollers. He lifted his rifle to his shoulder and squinted an eye down the barrel, which was pointed at a shadow. But from where he was, Austin could see what Narvel couldn't—that the gun was aimed at Henry-James.

If Henry-James moved, he was going to attract the attention of the Patty Rollers. If he didn't, he was going to take a shot from the gun of Narvel, who thought he was about to take a squirrel home for supper.

Austin couldn't get hold of a single thought—there were so many tearing in panic through his head. He clutched frantically at one.

"Soon as I grab Narvel, you get Henry-James and run—home!" he whispered.

He didn't wait to see if Charlotte agreed. He sprang out from behind the tree and shouted, "Narvel Guthrie, don't you shoot those Patty Rollers! They never did anything to you!"

Narvel jumped just as Austin grabbed him around the legs and tumbled him to the ground. Even as they fell, it crossed Austin's mind that the boy was like an iron pole. No wonder he gave Henry-James a run for his money in a fight.

Narvel rolled on top of Austin, pinning his arms to the ground. Austin grinned up at him. The gun had been tossed aside, and the Patty Rollers were crashing toward them through the underbrush. Everything was working out as if he'd planned it that way. He didn't dare look to see if Charlotte was escaping unnoticed with Henry-James.

"What in tarnation did you think you were doin', pointin' that gun at us?" Barnabas Brown demanded above them. "Come on, get off that boy."

When Narvel didn't, Irvin grabbed him by the back of his shirt collar and jerked him to his feet. Narvel kicked and squirmed, but Irvin held fast.

"Well?" Barnabas whined at him. "What have you got to say for yourself?"

"Nothin' till you let me go!" Narvel said tightly. "I ain't no Negro you can take home for money. Turn me loose!"

Austin could barely smother a smirk. *How does it feel, being treated the way you treat Henry-James?* he thought. He hoped Irvin didn't let go.

When he did, Narvel snatched himself away and brushed at his ragged flannel shirt as if it had been touched by smallpox.

"I wasn't doin' nothin' but huntin' a squirrel to eat!" he said.

"At this time of night?" Irvin growled. "Only a fool would do that!"

"Well, this fool ain't got no other time to do it," Narvel snapped at him. "I'm workin' all day just to pay the rent on our house—me and my daddy both. Only time I got to get a meal together's when I'm done with chores at our own place."

"Why can't your daddy hunt?"

"He's ailin'. Can't hardly put in a full day's work as it is. Not that it's any of your never mind."

That didn't even get a blink out of Barnabas. "What about your mama? Does she think she's too good to pick up a rifle or set a rabbit trap?"

"My mama done died a year ago," Narvel said. "Now if'n you heard enough of my private business, I'm gonna git me a squirrel 'fore them childrens starve to death."

Narvel didn't wait for an answer, but sneered down at Austin and turned on the heel of his boot and disappeared into the trees, back toward his house.

"You—nephew Ravenal," Irvin Ullmann said in his gravelly voice. "What are *you* doin' out here?"

"I told you!" Barnabas said shrilly. "That little cuffee was here. Why else would this one be stalkin' around?"

Irvin took a threatening step toward Austin.

"If you're talking about Henry-James," Austin said, "I don't know where he is, and I'm not breaking the law being out here. So if you'll excuse me, I'm going home."

"Does your uncle know you're out here?" Irvin said, narrowing his eyes until they nearly crossed.

"And does he know you're tangling with the likes of that white trash?" Barnabas put in.

Austin ignored them both and, turning his back, stomped away. He hoped they couldn't see that walking deeper into the forest in the pitch-black night was the last thing he wanted to do—or that their last two questions had sent fear skittering through his mind.

What if they do mention to Uncle Drayton that I was out here? What if they tell him I was talking to Narvel?

He clenched his hands with determination. It didn't matter. He'd think of something. After all, he was doing what was really right. He wasn't being a hypocrite like just about everybody else.

He had Jesus on his side.

He wished, however, that Jesus Himself—or somebody else brave—was there to show him the way out of the woods. His feet felt like blocks of lead as he put one heavily before the other and tried not to shrink from every shadow and rustling leaf. But when a stocky-shouldered silhouette stepped out from behind a sweet gum tree, Austin shrieked like a startled crow.

"It's jus' me, Massa Austin," Henry-James whispered. "Come on, we got to get you home."

It was a bleary-eyed Austin who slipped up the back stairs with Charlotte that night and a minute later crawled into bed beside Jefferson. He was just drifting off to sleep when it occurred to him to wonder whether anyone had remembered to leave Kady's note where Aunt Olivia or Uncle Drayton would find it. He didn't have to wonder long.

He woke up the next morning to the sound of a piercing, hysterical scream from the front hallway.

"Good heavens, Olivia, what is it?" he heard Uncle Drayton say.

Austin scrambled out of bed and met his mother and Charlotte in the hallway. Polly joined them a second later, neatly tucking her hair up under her ruffled nightcap.

"What's going on?" she whispered.

Austin pointed below, where it was silent for the moment. Leaning over the banister, he saw Uncle Drayton reading from a piece of paper with a ragged edge. Charlotte nudged Austin in the ribs.

"There is no need to fuss, Olivia," Uncle Drayton said. He creased the paper hard with his fingers and thrust it inside his waistcoat. His mouth was tightened into a line. "She seems to be safe at least."

Aunt Olivia took the handkerchief Mousie appeared with and dabbed at her eyes. "But this is dreadful, simply dreadful! I'm in the middle of planning her wedding for next week, and she's off hiding who knows where. Her gown will be ready for a fitting day after tomorrow!"

"She will be here," Uncle Drayton said. "If I have to dig up every acre of this parish, I will find her, and by heaven, she will be here!"

His heels clicked angrily across the wood floor as he stalked back to his library and slammed the door. Charlotte drew back from the banister. Her freckles were standing out.

"What was that all about?" Polly said.

Austin was afraid to open his mouth for fear everything in his mind would come spilling out. Polly looked at him suspiciously.

"Do you know anything about this, Austin?" she said.

"Austin," Sally Hutchinson said, "I'd like to speak to you in my room. Charlotte, why don't you join us. Polly, hurry and get dressed so you can find out what's happening downstairs and fill the rest of us in."

Polly seemed to like that idea and bustled off. Austin exchanged furtive looks with Charlotte as they followed Mother into her room.

"You two look as guilty as a pair of thieves," Austin's mother said when the door was closed. "This is too serious for you to be trying to do something alone. Tell me what you know."

Charlotte's face got whiter. Mother took her hand and pulled her close. "I can help, Charlotte," she said. "I may be a grown-up, but I'm not the enemy."

"I just don't want Kady to get into trouble," Charlotte said, her voice tiny. "Or Henry-James either."

Mother's eyebrows shot up. "Henry-James? What does he have to do with this?"

Charlotte looked helplessly at Austin, who for once couldn't think of anything to say.

Mother dropped Charlotte's hand and folded her arms. "Did you two follow that map last night?" she said. "And take Henry-James with you—off the plantation?"

"We didn't take him," Austin said. "He wouldn't let us go without him."

"Kady's all right, then? She has a decent place to stay?"

Austin grunted. "She isn't sleeping out in the swamp with the alligators, if that's what you mean."

"What are her plans?"

"She says she needs time to think," Austin said. "She thought if Uncle Drayton got word that she was safe, he'd leave her alone so she could decide what to do."

"It doesn't look like that plan is going to work," Mother said. "He's more determined than ever."

"He looked like he could drag her back by the hair!" Charlotte said.

"Just because she won't marry some stuffy soldier boy?"

"I think there's more to it than that," Mother said. "When we get upset over things we can't do anything about, we tend to point all our anger at something we think we can change."

Austin snorted. "That must be part of being a hypocrite."

But his mother didn't seem to be listening. She was absently stroking her chin with her eyes focused on the wall. Charlotte shifted from one foot to the other and toyed with the hem of her nightgown.

"You know," Mother said finally, "I can't help but think that if we're just honest with Uncle Drayton, we can bring Kady back here and talk about this together like reasonable people. No one has tried that yet." She looked at Charlotte. "I think you should tell your daddy where Kady is. I'll talk to him first and try to calm him down."

"No!" Austin cried.

"Austin, please."

"No, you don't understand! If Uncle Drayton knows where Kady is, then somebody else is gonna get in trouble, and then Henry-James will, too. We can't tell yet!"

Mother looked from one of them to the other. "You two have woven a tangled web this time, haven't you?"

"But it's a good web," Austin said. "We just need a little more time."

"How long before somebody gets caught in it, my love?" Mother said.

Austin didn't know. He didn't even know what the rest of the plan was. There was only one sure thing screaming in his head: *Uncle Drayton can't find out that the Guthries are hiding Kady until we're sure Narvel is going to leave Henry-James alone for good.*

And only Henry-James himself could help them figure out how *that* was going to happen.

"All right," Mother said with a sigh. "I'm going to give you until supper time. And then we're all going to Uncle Drayton together." She stood up. "In the meantime, I have a letter to mail."

"To Father?" Austin said.

"We'll talk about that later," she said. "I think you have enough to think about for now. Remember, by supper time."

Charlotte nodded woodenly as Austin led the way out of the room. In the hallway, she started to splinter.

"What are we gonna do?" she whispered. "Maybe we should tell Kady so she can find another place."

"Get dressed," Austin said. "We have to find Henry-James."

That was no easy task. There was no one but a fitfully-sleeping Bogie in the slave cabin, and Mousie said Uncle Drayton had ridden off alone on his horse. When they didn't find Henry-James in any of the shops or the stable or barnyard, they decided to split up. It was already getting toward noon.

"We'll try all the fields," Austin said. "They should be stopping for dinner in a little while. Maybe we'll find him then."

Austin bolted for the southeast tip of the rice fields while Charlotte took off for the northern end.

"We'll meet in the middle," she promised him.

There wasn't much going on in the fields now except for repairing the dikes and plowing under the stubble, so it was easy to sort through the thin crew of slaves who had their backs bowed to their work. None of them was Henry-James. The sun was trying to burn through a gray sky straight overhead when Austin reached the midway point and saw Charlotte running toward him, her heels kicking up her green cape.

"Did you find him?" Austin said.

She shook her head and gasped for her breath. "No," she said. "But I found Daddy Elias. He was all upset because Henry-James didn't even report to him for his tasks this morning."

"Didn't they have breakfast together in the cabin?"

"No. Bogie was doing *worse* when they got up, and Henry-James just got all 'flashed-eyed'—that's what Daddy 'Lias said—and he ran out of the cabin." Charlotte swallowed hard. "This is the worst part, Austin. He told Daddy 'Lias he had business to do—he was gonna find that boy that shot Bogie!"

"Narvel," Austin said. "He can't do that. It's gonna ruin everything!"

"Austin, this is getting scary. Maybe Aunt Sally was right—"

Austin jabbed his hands onto his hips. "Are you gonna turn into a chicken *now?*" he said. "After all this?"

Charlotte snapped her head up so hard that her hood fell back onto her shoulders. "I am *not* a chicken, Austin Hutchinson!" she said. "I just don't think I know everything in the world the way you think you do! I don't think I'm better than everybody else and don't need anybody to tell me what to do!"

Austin stared at her. "I don't do that," he said.

"You're doing it right now."

Austin felt stung. "I am not either," he said. "Go ahead, *you* think of how we're gonna find Henry-James."

Biting her lip, she looked up at the sky. "It's noon. He's probably going to the well for some water."

Austin snorted. "Not if he's out tracking down Narvel. Matter of fact, *I* bet he went to the dog-trot house."

"He wouldn't leave the plantation by himself—not with the Patty Rollers out," Charlotte said. She yanked her hood up onto her head. "I'm going to go look at the well."

His face still stinging as if he'd been slapped, Austin watched as she swept off. He forced himself to turn the other way, to head toward the narrow end of Rice Mill Pond and the forest. *Sometimes you have to do things by yourself when you know you're right*, he told himself. *It isn't easy being just about the only one who isn't a hypocrite.*

But it didn't make the angry, jabbing feeling in his backbone stop. He looked back over his shoulder, but Charlotte had already disappeared. He twisted to look at the woods again—and the memory of the previous night's events made him shiver.

Turning on his boot heel, he hurried after Charlotte. *She isn't going to find Henry-James at the well,* he thought, *and then I can talk her into going to the Guthries' with me.*

That felt better—at least a little.

He caught up with Charlotte just around the bend in the path that led to the well.

"Are you going to say 'I told you so' if he isn't here?" she said.

Before Austin could answer, they heard a shout from around the bend—a funny kind of shout, as if it were coming from inside a cave.

"That didn't sound like Henry-James," Austin said.

They listened, and the shout came again, louder this time and urgent-sounding.

"Help!" a voice clearly said. "Somebody get me out of here!"

Austin and Charlotte looked at each other for the tiniest part of a second before they tore off down the path. The shouting went on, growing more frenzied—so it was easy to tell the minute they rounded the bend that it was coming from inside the well.

Austin ran to the side and peered down. From out of the inky darkness came the whiny voice of Narvel Guthrie.

✜◦✜◦✜

$\mathcal{A}$ ustin's first reaction was, of course, a question. "How did you end up down there?" he said.

"How do you think?" Narvel said, his voice shivering. "That miserable darky friend of yours. I shoulda done him in at the cornhuskin' when I had the chance."

Austin grinned down at him. "Looks like he did you in instead. How did he do this?"

He peered closely at where Narvel was hanging, a good 10 feet below the top of the wall. The water bucket was gone, and Narvel was crouched in a barrel. Austin followed the ropes with his eyes and saw where Henry-James had cut the bucket off and tied the barrel in its place.

"Pretty smart of Henry-James," Austin said. "He knew that bucket would never hold you—lucky for you—"

"Yeah?" Narvel said. "Well, he ain't that smart. Them ropes will be frayin' pretty soon if somebody doesn't get me out of here."

Charlotte looked up at the pulley system. "Is that true?"

Austin nodded. "Yeah, it is. I guess we'd better turn the crank and get him out."

"It's gonna take two of ya," Narvel called up to them.

"I *know*," Austin said. "I've read all about this stuff."

Narvel's grunt resounded through the well.

Austin jumped up and caught hold of the crank to pull it down so Charlotte could get her hands on it, too. It wouldn't budge.

"I told ya it would take both of ya!" Narvel shouted.

Austin ignored him. "I'll get up on the side so I can get better leverage. In case you don't know, leverage is when—"

"Just do it!" Narvel fairly screamed.

Austin grinned at Charlotte. "He isn't so tough now, is he?"

It took two tries, but Austin managed to get himself up onto the well's stone wall. As he stood up and crept toward the crank, the world began to wobble.

"Are you all right?" Charlotte said. "Do you want me to do it? I get up there all the time."

"No," Austin said. His voice came out sharper than he'd expected. It made even him jerk. He grabbed for the crank and held on.

"Are you sure, Austin?" Charlotte said. She shielded her eyes with her hand to look up at him. "Maybe I should go get help."

"No," Austin said through his teeth. He jerked his head toward Narvel. "You know why."

Charlotte twisted her mouth and watched. Austin moved both hands to the handle part of the crank and pulled. He could hear the rope creaking, but nothing moved.

"Put your back into it!" Narvel shouted. "You can't do it with just those spindly little arms!"

"I'm coming up there with you!" Charlotte said.

"No, I can do it!" Austin could feel his face throbbing, his back jabbing, his head spinning.

Hunching up his shoulders and scrunching up his face, he squeezed the crank handle tight and yanked down with everything he had in him. The crank lurched—with a lash so hard it threw Austin backward.

His momentum pulled his hands off the handle, and he felt himself careen—down, wild, out of control.

"Austin!" he heard Charlotte scream.

The back of his neck hit something hard, and his arms were wrenched upward. His legs dangled down, but he stopped falling. Somebody was tugging hard at his arms.

"Stop moving!" Narvel shouted in his ear. "If you stop moving, I can haul you in here."

Only then did Austin realize he was hanging on the outside of the barrel, facing the inside wall of the well. Narvel had hold of his arms—and he was the only thing keeping Austin from plunging to the black water below.

"Be still!" Narvel barked again.

Austin stopped kicking his legs and stopped breathing.

"I'm gonna turn loose of this arm," Narvel said, squeezing Austin's right bicep. "You swing around and grab hold of the barrel so's you're facin' me."

"Don't let go!" Austin cried.

"You ain't gonna fall if'n you do it quick," Narvel said. "I'll catch you if you start to go."

"No, you won't. You'll let me fall!"

"If I'da wanted you to fall, I'da let you go on and fail. I'm the one caught you in the first place!"

Austin craned his neck to look up. "Go get help, Lottie!" he shouted.

But Charlotte had already disappeared.

"Quit bein' stupid and do what I say," Narvel said. "I'm gonna let go on the count o' three. You swing around soon as I do."

Austin desperately nodded his head.

"One, two—"

"No, don't!"

"Three—"

Austin's arm came loose. Without even having to think about

it, he swung across himself and grabbed onto the barrel. Narvel's hands were back on his arms almost before Austin knew he'd let go. Austin breathed into the side of the barrel.

"All right, you done that," Narvel said. "Now, pull your leg up so I can get your armpits over the edge here. Then you can pull yourself in."

"Inside the barrel?" Austin said. He hardly recognized his own voice. It was twittering like a frightened bird.

"You got a better idea?" Narvel said.

"No," Austin said.

"Then hike that leg up."

Austin had no idea what he was talking about, but obediently he pulled his leg up against the side of the barrel. As he did, Narvel pulled hard, and slowly he came up until the barrel was tucked under his arms.

"I'll keep pullin' and you keep climbin'," Narvel said.

He gave an iron tug, and Austin clawed like a crab with his legs. His chest was up on the side of the barrel, then his stomach. Narvel plastered himself thin against the side.

"Keep crawlin' like you're gonna go out the other side," Narvel said. "Just till you get your legs in."

"Why?"

"Because you're gonna be upside down in here if'n you don't—and we all know you don't like that."

Narvel gave a chuckle. Austin felt his face burn, but he reached out with his arms and grabbed onto the other side of the barrel. He could feel Narvel hanging on to his middle as he pulled his legs in and dropped them to the bottom of the barrel. His forehead was an inch from Narvel's nose.

"It ain't a plantation mansion," Narvel said, "but it's all we got."

Austin tried to twist himself around.

"What are you doing?" Narvel said.

"I'm turning around so I don't have to look at you!"

"There's no room. Quit squirmin' around or you'll send this whole thing down. You want that?"

"No!" Austin said.

"Then be still."

Austin was. He positioned his eyes on the dirty front of Narvel's shirt and tried to get his heart to be a little calmer, too. It was thumping like a rabbit's foot.

"You think I like lookin' at your Ravenal face any better'n you like lookin' at mine?" Narvel said.

Austin brought his eyes up sharply to meet Narvel's. "Why should you mind looking at me? I never did anything to you! Matter of fact, I even made it so my uncle wouldn't find out that you're hiding my cousin at your house!"

"Sure, in return for me promisin' not to hurt your precious little darky. And then he up and dumps me in a well!"

"Because you shot his dog, that's why."

"I never did no such thing!"

Austin rolled his eyes. "You're not only a hypocrite, you're a liar, too."

Narvel drew his face into its between-the-eyebrows scowl. "What is that word you keep sayin' all the time?" Narvel said.

"What, *hypocrite?*"

"Yeah."

"Funny you don't know what it means, seeing how you *are* one."

"I'll decide that," Narvel said. "What is it?"

"It's a person who says he believes one thing, but he acts some other way."

Narvel's frown grew deeper, as if he were actually thinking that over. His green eyes took on a light.

"That pretty much describes you if you ask me," he said.

"Me!" Austin said. His voice crackled. "I'm not a hypocrite! I would never do some of the things you've done!"

"Like what?"

"Like the way you cheated in the wrestling match and lied about it."

"Had to lie," Narvel said.

"Nobody *has* to lie," Austin said. "Jesus doesn't like it when we lie."

"So, He doesn't like it that you're lying to cover up for Kady."

"That's different."

"Still a lie. At least I admit it. You don't—so I guess that makes you the hypocrite, not me."

"Huh," Austin said. "I bet you won't admit you did all those things to Henry-James to get him in trouble."

"Sure I will. I'll own up to things you don't even know I done."

"Like what?"

"Like that trap in the woods." Narvel cocked his lip. " 'Course it was supposed to get the darky, not you."

"You did not either set that trap!" Austin said. "You're not smart enough."

Narvel's face went red all the way up his high forehead. "You think you're the only one that's smart?" he said. "Does *Jesus* like that about you?"

Austin's mind scrambled. "All right, if you set the trap, how did you figure it out?"

"I just thought it up. I don't *have* to read about everything in books."

"So did you just think up shooting Bogie, too?" Austin said. He could feel his cheeks stinging again.

"I didn't shoot the dog," Narvel said. "If we can't eat it, I don't kill it, simple as that."

"Now who's a hypocrite? You tell me I'm a liar and won't admit it—"

"I ain't lyin'!"

Narvel gave his neck a snap to get his hair back and smacked his head against the side of the barrel. It swayed, and Austin clutched the top with both hands. Narvel looked up and studied the pulley, so far above them.

"This ain't gonna hold much longer. Where did that girl go for help, Charleston?"

Austin breathed hard until the barrel stopped rocking. His heart kept pummeling the inside of his chest.

"Yer scared, ain't ya?" Narvel said.

"No!"

"Then you are a hypocrite—preachin' to me about lyin' and then standin' there tellin' me you ain't about to pee yer pants when I can see yer eyes goin' wild and yer lip all broke out in a sweat."

Austin licked his upper lip and tasted the salt. "All right, I'm scared! Are you happy now? Who wouldn't be scared? We're hanging in a well in a barrel on ropes that aren't strong enough to hold us. And if we do fall, we're gonna go 30 feet into water. And I don't know about you, but I can't swim—which doesn't really matter because the *fall* will probably kill us!"

"Well, would you listen to that," Narvel said. "A real regular human bein', just like me."

"No, I am *not* just like you," Austin said. He tried to cool his voice. "I pray all the time. I try to do what's right. If I lie, it's because somebody else is being stupid and they . . . I don't know, they force me to."

"Like I said, sounds just like me. 'Cept I don't pray."

"You can sure tell that," Austin said.

"And you wanna know why?" Narvel said.

Austin didn't actually, but the storm brewing in the boy's green eyes made him nod his head anyway. "Why?" he said.

"Because of people like you, who talk 'n' talk about how good they are because they believe in Jesus, but they're so busy tellin' everybody else how bad they are, they ain't got time to look at theirselves. I don't wanna pray to no God that's gonna make me think I'm better'n everybody else."

"I don't think I'm better than everybody else!" Austin said.

"You sure act like it. I'd be takin' a bath myself 'fore I told somebody else how dirty *they* was."

Austin opened his mouth to answer—and closed it again. He'd heard this before, only in a different way. And it hadn't stung before like it did now. He would have remembered that.

"We're both sinners, far as I can tell," Narvel said. "So I don't reckon you got any right to be judgin' me."

"I can't throw a stone at you," Austin said slowly. "Not unless I never did anything wrong."

Narvel nodded. "Yeah. Somethin' like that. Besides, the way I figure it, I do the best I can, but sometimes I got to get the other feller 'fore he gets me worse. And if you say you don't do that, then you *are* one of them hippopotamuses or whatever you call 'em."

"Hypocrite," Austin said absently. He pretended to look up at the pulley, but his mind was someplace else—down on Slave Street where the words were crackling out of Daddy Elias's mouth.

"I reckon you didn't know you got a beam in your eye, Massa Austin. . . . Not to worry none 'bout the mote in that white boy's eye till you take care o' that beam you totin' around."

Austin could almost feel his heart sagging. Usually when he figured something out, it sang through him like a victory tune. But figuring this out didn't feel good at all.

"Nah," Narvel was saying. "I don't believe in Jesus because no matter how hard we try, we still got bad. I reckon bad is a whole lot bigger than anybody 'round here."

Austin wasn't sure what to think now. The only thing that came to his mind as he stared at Narvel was something else Daddy

Elias had said: *"He got a nasty heart somebody done give him."*

Austin looked back up at the pulley—and prayed the first real prayer he'd prayed in a long time. *Jesus? Did somebody give me a nasty heart? If they did, could You please let me know so I can get rid of it? I feel awful.*

"Catfish!" Narvel suddenly shouted. "Do you see what I see, smart boy?"

Austin jerked his head and tried to focus where Narvel's eyes were going, up to the pulley. As soon as he saw it, he knew what Narvel was talking about. Even from here, he could see that the rope was fraying.

The barrel was hanging by a few dozen threads.

Chapter Sixteen

"We have to get out of here—now," Austin said.

"I figured that much out for my own self," Narvel said. "But I'm gonna need you to tell me how, seein' how you got all the answers."

"I don't have all the answers," Austin said miserably. "I wish you'd quit saying that."

"I only say it 'cause you keep remindin' me."

"We don't have time for this! We have to think about getting out!" He stared up at the rope, heart slamming, and rubbed his sweaty hands up and down his pant legs. "Maybe one of us could climb the rope and pull the other one out."

"The only one of us knows how to climb a rope is me, and I done thought of that already. Won't work."

"Why not?" Austin said.

"We start jerkin' that rope, it's gonna snap for sure."

Austin swallowed and studied the pulley some more. "So somebody has to pull the rope from below where it's breaking."

"Somebody like who?" Narvel said.

"Charlotte will come back with help," Austin said. He tried to sound hopeful. *It's sure taking her a long time, though,* he thought. *She probably can't find the right people. I'd take Uncle Drayton himself right now!*

He sighed hard and tried to straighten his shoulders. It was hard with Narvel pressed up against him.

"Don't move," Narvel snapped. "You're swingin' the barrel. It's gonna hit the side."

"Sorry," Austin said.

He was starting to feel like the walls were moving in on them. Pretty soon they'd be able to touch the stones sticking out.

"Hey!" Austin said.

"You don't gotta yell. I'm right here."

"What if we *did* swing the barrel—so we could grab on to one of those big stones that sticks out on the side? There're enough of them. One of us—well, *you*—could climb up."

"I ain't a spider!" Narvel said.

"I'm not a pickle either, but here I am sitting in a barrel!"

"Where do you get these ideas?"

"I don't know," Austin said, "but it's better than just sitting here waiting to fall."

"Now I *know* I'm smarter than you," Narvel said. "If ya want to climb up the side, climb up the side. I ain't gonna stop ya."

Austin looked doubtfully at the stone wall again. There *were* a lot of rocks sticking out, and it wasn't wet there where the water never touched. But he could barely climb a tree, much less scale a wall.

"You're right," Austin said. "I can't do that. We'll have to think of something else."

"There ain't nothin' else."

"Then Charlotte will come. She wouldn't just leave me down here."

"Huh," Narvel said. "She might. She's probably just as sick of your mouth as I am."

Yet again, Austin was stung. *I don't think I know everything in the world the way you think you do!* That's what she'd said to him.

Austin patted his mouth with his hand and blinked hard.

"Oh, for Pete's sake," Narvel growled. "If you're gonna cry, I ain't stayin'. I hate crybabies."

"I do, too," Austin said in a choked-back voice.

"All right. Start swayin', but easy now. If that rope breaks, ain't nobody never gonna get us out."

"You're gonna try climbing the wall?"

"Yeah, and I ain't gonna be no hippo-whatever 'bout it neither. I'm 'bout to lose my breakfast. Come on, start rockin'."

With their eyes glued to the fraying rope above them, they swayed gently from one side of the barrel until it began to swing toward the side.

"Just a little harder," Austin said.

"I can see that," Narvel said.

They put their shoulders into it and the barrel swung—once, twice—and the third time bumped the wall.

"All right, next time you let go and grab," Austin said.

Narvel nodded. His face looked cold and still. He hadn't been joking, Austin thought. He was scared.

"Ready?" Austin said.

Narvel leaned into the swing, and so did Austin. Three good sways and they thudded against the wall. Narvel grabbed hold of a stone with two hands and the barrel stopped.

"Good!" Austin cried. "There's another one just above your head. Get that one with one hand—"

But Narvel's hands suddenly came free and the barrel swung back into the well, almost hitting the opposite wall.

"They slipped off!" Narvel cried.

"Let's try again!"

"You have to hold on, too, until I get out of the barrel. Our weight is pullin' me back."

"All right, let's go!"

Austin was jittery from toenails to hair roots. He didn't dare look up at the rope again. *We gotta keep hoping,* he told himself.

Once again they swayed the barrel until it hit the wall. Both Austin and Narvel clung to stones that stuck out. One of Austin's was tilted upward and was so easy to hang on to that he almost tried to climb out of the barrel himself. But Narvel was already out up to his ankles, and it was hard to hold on by himself.

"All right, turn loose!" Narvel called out.

Austin let go, and the barrel swayed loosely back out into the hole. Austin suddenly felt naked and small in the barrel alone.

Narvel, in the meantime, was flat against the wall, his feet hooked on to two jutting stones, his hands clinging to two more. His cheek hugged the side, and he didn't move.

"What's the matter?" Austin said.

"I can't look up," Narvel said. His voice was thin and had none of its growl.

"Why not?"

"I'm afraid I'll fall, all right? You try goin' up a wall and see how brave you are!"

"All right, if you can't look up, I'll tell you where the next stones are. You can just follow my directions and feel until you find them."

There was a long pause before Narvel said, "All right."

Austin scanned the wall carefully. "Take your left hand," he said, "and go up about two hand prints' worth."

Narvel did.

"Do you feel that?"

"Yeah, I got it. Now what?"

"Take your right foot to the right about where your knee is now."

Slowly, foot by foot and hand by hand, Austin directed Narvel toward the top. He forced himself not to look up at the rope but kept his eyes nailed to the stones sticking out. The barrel never moved, but Narvel did, until one more set of holds would bring him close enough to climb out.

"What now?" Narvel said.

"You're almost there," Austin said.

"Then tell me what to do next, 'cause my hands 'bout to rub raw."

Austin stared hard at the wall, and a pang rose in his throat.

"Well?" Narvel said.

"Let me look," Austin said.

"Hurry!"

I wish I could, Austin thought frantically. But there were no stones jutting out even close to where Narvel was. He would have to lean far to either side to grab on to anything, and he might not be able to reach—not without falling.

"Come on, boy!" Narvel cried. "I can't hold on much longer!"

"How far can you reach out to your right?" Austin said.

"What? What are you sayin'—go sideways?"

"How far?" Austin said. He was trying to keep the fear out of his voice, but as soon as it was in the air, he could tell Narvel heard it. The boy stiffened and turned his head as far as he dared.

"There ain't no handholds up above me?" Narvel said.

"No, but don't give up. Just reach way to the right—"

"I can't!"

"You have to!"

"I can't reach, and I can't hold on! I got to get out of here!"

"You have to try!"

"Good Lordy, Miz Lottie, that rope about broke clean through!"

"Henry-James!" Austin screamed. "Henry-James, help!"

Three faces shot out over the wall above him. None of them saw the figure flattened against the wall. They saw only a suddenly shaking Austin.

"He left you down there by yourself!" Charlotte cried.

"How did he get out?" said Polly.

Henry-James was already hoisting himself up onto the wall.

"Don't touch the crank!" Austin shouted. "You'll break the rope! You have to get Narvel out first!"

"Narvel?" Charlotte said.

All eyes followed Austin's pointing finger, and they gasped as one.

"Help me, please!" Narvel said. His voice was barely there, and Austin could see his hands going white in their desperate attempt to hold on.

"If you reach down, you can get him. He doesn't have anyplace else to grab on!" Austin cried.

Henry-James jumped from the wall and hurried to a place above Narvel. He thrust his hand down, but his fingers barely touched Narvel's.

"Get something he can grab on to!" Austin shouted.

Polly whipped off her cape and handed it to Henry-James, who lowered it down until it was well within Narvel's reach.

For a long 10 seconds, Narvel stared at it.

"Grab on to it!" Austin shouted at him. "There's three of them up there—they can pull you up."

"Is it the darky?" Narvel said.

"What difference does it make?"

"I don't want him touchin' me!"

There was a creaking sound. Henry-James jerked his head toward the rope.

"You better decide, Massa Narvel," Henry-James said. "'Cause if'n you doesn't want to be rescued, I'm gonna save Massa Austin. He's 'bout to fall!"

Narvel snatched at the cape with both hands. "Pull!" he cried.

Three faces turned red as the children tugged the cape with Narvel on it up to the top of the wall. He slapped his hands onto the stones and hoisted himself up on the wall.

"What are you doing?" Polly cried.

Austin watched, his heart pounding, his hands clutched white on the sides of the barrel, as Narvel ran along the wall as if it were a three-foot sidewalk.

"The rope's breaking!" Polly screamed.

Austin looked up and felt his eyes freeze in their sockets. The last thread of the rope snapped, the barrel lurched, and Austin heard himself scream. The barrel hit the side of the well with a crack.

"Help me hold the rope! Come on, everybody, grab on!" Narvel shouted.

There was a tangle of cries and pounding feet above. The barrel lurched and jerked—and then was still. Austin sucked in his breath to keep from throwing up.

"You hold on just like that," he heard Narvel say. "And don't nobody let go."

"Where do you think you're going?" Polly said.

"I'll be right back. Just hold on like I told you."

To his horror, Austin heard footsteps running away from the well.

"What's happening?" he cried out again.

No one's face appeared over the side. He could only hear Henry-James calling out to him.

"You all right, Massa Austin?"

"I want to get out of here is all. What is going on?"

"That Narvel boy done tol' us where to hol' on to this here rope—and then he run off."

"He *said* he's coming right back," Austin heard Polly say. "Personally, I don't believe him."

"But why wouldn't he have just run off when we first pulled him out?" Charlotte said.

"'Cause he knowed if'n we was holding on to Massa Austin,

we wouldn't turn loose to run off chasin' him," Henry-James said.

"And we can't get more help," Charlotte said. Austin could hear the tremble in her voice.

And he also heard something else—his own voice inside reminding him: *I promise I'm going to be different now. I'm not going to throw any more stones.* He bit back a whimper and squeezed his eyes shut.

"Don't worry," he called up to his friends. "I think he'll be back."

There was a thinking silence.

"I thought you said he was a lying little cheater," Polly said.

"He is—sometimes," Austin said. "But then, we all are."

"I beg your pardon!" Polly said, voice rising like a flute.

" 'Scuse me, Massa Austin, but that ain't true."

"All right!" Another voice pushed its way in between theirs.

Austin let out a long breath. Narvel was back.

"What on earth is that?" Polly said.

"What's what?" Austin called up. "Somebody tell me what's happening!"

"Can't stand it when you ain't in charge, can ya, smart boy?" Narvel said. "You just hush up and let us work."

Austin stretched his neck up until he felt like a turkey while everyone above went on about whatever it was they were doing. But as Narvel barked out orders, Austin figured it out.

"We're gonna attach that broke rope to this here pulley down here."

"Are we strong enough to hold on to it?"

"Yes'm, Miz Lottie. We ain't gonna let Massa Austin fall, no sirree."

"Where did you get this contraption anyway?"

"Up in a tree, I reckon, Miz Polly."

"Well, what on earth was it doing in a tree?"

"You ask more questions than yer cousin," Narvel said. "You

sure you ain't brother 'n' sister? Come on, it's ready."

Narvel's high forehead appeared over the top of the well wall. Even from the barrel, Austin could see his green eyes sparkling as if he were playing his favorite game.

"We're about to pull you out, thanks to me," he said. "You just stay right in the middle of that there barrel, and don't bounce around none."

Austin said, "Just hurry."

"You ready, Massa Austin?"

Austin straightened himself in the middle of the barrel and called up a yes. Rope began to creak and children began to grunt and wood scraped on stone. And the barrel began to rise.

Austin held on, eyes open, and prayed. *Please, Jesus, I won't be a hypocrite anymore. Just, please, let me get out of here.*

For a fanciful moment, Austin thought Jesus Himself was pulling him up.

Until the cranking stopped and more screaming started.

"The wall's fraying the rope!" Polly cried.

Black hands appeared at the top of the wall and grabbed on to the rope. Then two pairs of small white ones showed up. And then Narvel's face. Austin latched his own hands around a stone and stared up at them.

"How bad is it?" he said.

"Bad," Narvel said. The game-sparkle had fizzled out, and his green eyes were wet with fear.

"Do something!" Polly cried. "It's hard to hold on like this!"

"I don't *know* what to do!"

"Get the cape!" Charlotte cried.

Narvel ducked down and came back with the brown velvet cape. He flung it over the side, and Austin grabbed at it. But the barrel had sunk so far that he couldn't touch it—no matter how hard he stretched, no matter how far down Narvel reached.

"Austin! Try harder! You have to get it!" Charlotte's voice was nothing more than sobs.

Beside it, Polly's cried like a kitten. "Just a little farther—come on!"

"What are we going to *do?*" Charlotte said.

"I'll run get my daddy!" Narvel said.

"No, wait!"

They all looked down at Austin with terrified eyes.

"Just listen," Austin said. "You just have to get the rope away from the wall so it won't rub anymore. If Henry-James hangs on to the rope below where it's frayed, you can pull me up far enough to reach the cape."

"How we do that, Massa Austin?" Henry-James said. "How we keep that rope from touchin'?"

Austin's mind was racing again, and his hope was bubbling to the top. "Something soft," he said. "You can't use the cape because you'll need that—"

"Too bad you didn't wear petticoats today, Polly," Charlotte said.

"I'll tell you what I did wear."

There was a funny little gasp from Charlotte, and something dark auburn and curly appeared on top of the wall.

"What's that?" Austin said.

"It's my hairpiece," Polly said. "It's going to be ruined, but I think a man likes a woman who is willing to make sacrifices."

"Hush up and hold that rope!" Narvel cried. "Come on, I'll start crankin'!"

✝•✝•✝

Chapter Seventeen

With Henry-James gripping the rope below its frayed part with both hands, Polly making sure the hairpiece stayed in place on the wall, and Narvel cranking the handle of his pulley, the barrel slowly began to scrape its way up again. Austin prayed, *Please, I won't be a hypocrite anymore— ever. I promise.*

"I think he's close enough now!" Polly said.

The cape came over the side, and Austin grabbed at it, clutching it against his chest. Above, Narvel and Polly tugged on the other end. He was connected to them again.

"Scoot up so's yer hangin' on with yer legs, too," Narvel told him.

With muscles he didn't even know he had, Austin squeezed the soft cloth in his fists and pulled himself up until his legs were wrapped around the cape.

"I'm ready!" he cried.

Stones scraped his knuckles, and dampness oozed into his trousers at the knees, but Austin didn't care. He could feel the light at the top of the well almost reaching down to him.

"My hands are slipping!" Polly cried.

"Let go of the rope and help us!" Narvel shouted. "He's out of the barrel—turn it loose!"

Austin's heart slammed at his chest, but as he clawed at the cape, he felt the tug of more hands—Charlotte's and Henry-James's.

"You almost there, Massa Austin," Henry-James called to him. His voice was close, the light was close, the top was close.

And then Austin was there. Being hauled over the side. Tumbling to the ground. Being covered with the cape and the hugs and the warm breath of his friends.

"I'm cold," he said. His lips were quivering so much that he could hardly make them move.

"We must get him back to the Big House," Polly said, using her plantation mistress voice.

"You keep Mama occupied while I sneak him up the back stairs," Charlotte said.

"I don't want to sneak in," Austin said.

Charlotte's eyes widened. "But why?"

"I can't be a hypocrite."

"Here we go again," Narvel said. "I heard this already. I'm goin' home."

"Wait," Austin said. He struggled to sit up with the cape wrapped around him. "We have to talk first. I promised God."

"I didn't," Narvel said. But he crossed his arms and stuck his hands into his armpits and waited.

Austin looked at Henry-James. "You have to stop this fighting with Narvel. I know you're mad because he shot Bogie—"

"I didn't shoot no dog!"

"—but putting him down the well was just as bad."

Henry-James set his lips and looked sullenly at the ground.

"Henry-James didn't do it, Austin," Charlotte said. "Well, he *did*, but only because when he got here, Narvel was waiting with the barrel and tried to put *him* in it. Tell him, Henry-James."

Henry-James's black eyes flashed as he looked up at Narvel. "Onliest way I could keep from bein' lowered in there my own self was to rassle him into that there barrel and run. I come lookin' for you—"

"While we were looking for you!" Austin said. "Is that true, Narvel?"

Narvel shrugged. "Sure, I'll admit it. But I'm also the one that got you out."

"But he wouldn't even have been in there if it hadn't been for you!" Polly said. She tossed her now curl-less head. "You deserved what you got, after what you did to Bogie."

"I keep on tellin' ya, I didn't shoot the gol-durn dog!"

"Why will you admit everything else and not that?" Austin said. "We know you did it. Henry-James says the gun you were hunting with the other night was the same one that wounded Bogie."

"You think I'm the only one knows how to shoot the thing?" Narvel said.

"But you knew we were going hunting that day," Austin said. "You heard us talking when you set the trap."

"I heard ya. But I didn't do it. I ain't that low."

"I don't know," Polly said. "You're pretty low."

"All I want to hear is Narvel and Henry-James promising to stop this feud," Austin said.

"'Scuse me for sayin', Massa Austin," Henry-James said. "But he done made that promise before, and he done gone back on his word."

"That's only because I ain't never known a darky yet I could trust," Narvel said. "When I heard he was comin' after me, I decided to get there first."

"I wasn't gonna do nothin' to you," Henry-James said, his thick mouth drooping miserably. "'Cept tell you my dog gonna die—just so's you'd feel bad as I do."

"Naw, he won't die," Narvel said.

Their heads snapped toward him.

"Sometime they just takes a while to heal," he said. "We had us a pup we done give up for dead, and then a week later he lifted his head and just started a-sniffin'."

There was a surprised quiet. Austin broke it. "So, do you both promise?" he said.

"I ain't never done nothin' to him, and I never will," Henry-James said.

Narvel narrowed his eyes. "Like I said, I ain't never known a darky I could trust. But long as he don't do nothin' to me, I won't do nothin' to him." He shrugged. "I'm goin' home. I'm freezin' my backside off."

"Really!" Polly said, hand to chest. "There are ladies present!"

"One more thing before you go," Austin said. "We have to talk about Kady."

Polly's eyebrows went up like an ant's antennae. "What about Kady?"

Charlotte inched nervously toward Austin. "We have to make her promise, too," she whispered.

"Who, me?" Polly said. "Promise what?" She put her hands on her hips. "I have a right to know. I helped save you, too!"

Austin shifted his eyes away from Charlotte. "Kady's hiding at Narvel's house."

"Austin!" Charlotte said.

Polly put her hand to her mouth. "Oh," she said. "How . . . interesting."

"It's good enough," Narvel said huffily. "She's got a place to sleep." He cut his gaze to Austin, then nodded toward Polly. "She ain't gonna tell, is she?"

"Don't worry about me telling," Polly said, smoothing her hands down over her skirt. "The longer Kady stays gone, the better my chances are with Garrison."

Charlotte rolled her eyes.

Austin shook his head. "But I think we *should* tell Uncle Drayton. Only we'll have Narvel tell Kady we're going to so she can decide whether she wants to come home or keep running."

"But why, Austin?" Charlotte said. She was gnawing fiercely at her lip.

"Because I can't be a hypocrite," Austin said. "I promised."

"I think I'd rather be dropped to the bottom of that well than make a promise like that," Narvel said. His eyes were snapping. "What's gonna happen to my family now?"

"Don't worry," Austin said. "My mother is gonna help us. She won't let anything happen to you."

"She don't hire the help," Narvel said. He flipped his hair back, only to have it fall stubbornly down over his high forehead. "I'll tell Kady if you want me to, but I can't help what my daddy does when he finds out you done squealed like a pig to Mr. Ravenal."

"What you talkin' 'bout?" Henry-James said. He edged toward Narvel, eyes flashing.

"My daddy done seen a lot of trouble in his life," Narvel said. "He's pretty tired of it gettin' him. He's startin' to make some of his own trouble these days."

Austin rubbed the nervous sweat off his hands on his shirt front and looked straight at Narvel. "Just go home and tell Kady, like we said. And you just tell your daddy—"

"I don't tell my daddy nothin'," Narvel said. His eyes clouded and he looked away.

Austin knew then where Narvel's nasty heart came from.

Narvel hurried off, and Charlotte tugged at Austin's sleeve. "Please, Austin," she said. "Let's not tell Daddy."

"My mother's gonna help us," Austin said.

"But why did you change your mind?"

"You made me."

"Me?"

"You and Daddy Elias—and Narvel."

"You can't listen to him! He's bad!"

"Some ways he is, some ways not. He said the same thing you did."

"He did not either."

"Yes, he did. He said I act like I know everything and that I think I'm better than everybody else."

"I didn't mean that, Austin—honest."

"Maybe not," Austin said. "But it was true. That's being a hypocrite, and I can't do it anymore because I promised God if I got out of the well I wouldn't."

"I don't understand," she said. Her eyes filled up. "I'm so scared if we tell Daddy, something terrible is going to happen."

Austin raked his sweaty hands through his hair. "Me, too," he said. "Sometimes he acts nice and I think he's the best man in the world next to my father. And then sometimes, he's so mean. I'm sorry, Lottie, but sometimes I don't like him at all."

She looked sadly at her hands, and Austin sagged. *If it's so right*, he thought, *why does it feel so bad?* It was definitely one of those times when he didn't like Uncle Drayton at all.

And then like a candle flickering back to life, something occurred to him.

"Maybe we're wrong, Lottie," he said.

She looked up. "About telling?"

"No, about your father. If there's good in Narvel—you know, like how he feeds his brothers and sisters and rescued me from the well—then there's a whole *lot* of good in your daddy. Maybe this will be one of the good times. Maybe we have to hope and pray for that."

"Oh, no!"

They both twisted toward the well. Polly was leaning over it, so far that her feet came off the ground.

Austin made a dive for her and yanked her back by the skirt.

"Stop it, Boston!" Polly cried. "I was trying to see my hair-piece. It fell in!"

Austin stood cautiously on tiptoe and gave the well a wary peek. Floating on the dark water and sinking fast was a furry lump. Austin gulped to keep from laughing, but a guffaw erupted anyway and echoed through the well like a hundred Austins—all needing very badly to throw themselves on the ground and howl.

"It isn't funny!" Polly said, stomping her foot and looking not at all like a plantation mistress. "I was counting on that hair-piece!"

"I can't help it!" Austin said. "It's like it just . . . jumped off!"

Charlotte, too, began to giggle, and even Henry-James broke into a gap-toothed smile. Polly snatched up her cape and stomped off to the path. A stump-shaped figure careened around the bend and nearly knocked her down.

"Tot!" Polly said. "I told you to stay at the Big House and make excuses for us."

"I can't think of no more, Miz Polly!" Tot shrieked in her fin-gernail-scraping voice. "Missus says if'n marse come home 'fore you does, you all gonna wish you'd *stayed* gone!"

Tot's eyes threatened to leap from their sockets. Polly looked frantically at the rest of them. "We'd better go," she said. "And let me do the talking," she added. "I'm the only one of us Mama trusts."

"But don't be a hypocrite," Austin said as they followed her down the path.

"It was surely easier when you *were* one," Polly said.

Everything seemed to happen at once when they got back to the Big House. No sooner had the children poured out their story to Sally Hutchinson in her room than Jefferson reported from the window—where he had gone to pout because he hadn't been in-cluded in the adventure—that Uncle Drayton was coming up the drive on his horse. There was no time for changing minds. They stormed down the stairs in a mass, leaving Jefferson upstairs, squalling, with Tot.

They pounced on Uncle Drayton the moment he opened the door.

"Take your coat 'n' hat, Marse Drayton?" Henry-James said.

"Drayton, we need to speak to you right away," Austin's mother said.

"And Daddy, you need to listen very carefully," Polly put in.

"May I take a breath first?" Uncle Drayton said. He looked gray and weary, and his voice was impatient.

Austin groaned inside. This didn't look good, but there was no turning back now.

"What is all this?" Aunt Olivia said, bustling out from the drawing room with a russet silk gown over her arm. "Charlotte Ann, where have you been? I've been waiting all afternoon for you to try on your dress for the wedding. How am I to put on this event with no cooperation from the rest of you?"

"Livvy," said Mother, "that is exactly what we're all here to talk about. Drayton, may we sit down with you, please?"

"It doesn't look as if I have much choice," he said curtly. He looked at the crowd in front of him and nodded toward the dining room instead of the library.

They followed, with Aunt Olivia still trilling, "I demand to know the meaning of all this!"

"I don't know the meaning of it, Livvy," Mother said as she sat across from her brother. "I only know the story—you two will have to decide what to do with it."

"What story?" Uncle Drayton said. "And where is Josephine? I want some cocoa."

"I'll fetch it, Marse Drayton," Henry-James said.

"No, I think you should stay, Henry-James," Mother said. "You're so much a part of this."

"So now you're in charge of the slaves, Sally?" Uncle Drayton said.

She cocked an eyebrow at him. He sank back in his chair and ran his hand across his hair. "I'm sorry," he said. "I've been riding around all afternoon in this miserable dampness, and I still haven't found my daughter."

"I know where she is, Drayton," Mother said. "That's what I want to tell you."

Uncle Drayton's chair scraped back so sharply that Austin jumped, and Charlotte and Polly grabbed his arm on either side.

"Where?" Uncle Drayton said. "So help me I'll bring her back bound and gagged if I have to."

"I'm not going to tell you a thing until you stop that kind of talk," Mother said. "Why don't you just sit down and for once in your life just *listen*."

"Mercy!" Aunt Olivia said, clutching both of her chins. "Drayton, you do not have to allow her to speak to you like that."

"Talk, Sally," Uncle Drayton said.

Austin's mother did. She told the story from beginning to end, just the way the children had told it to her. Uncle Drayton sat with his eyes fixed on her and his hands folded on the table in front of him.

"Kady doesn't really want to be away from Canaan Grove and her family," Mother said when she was through. "She just wants to be allowed to choose what she does with the rest of her life. I think every human being wants that."

"It doesn't look to me as if Kady is ready to choose," Uncle Drayton said.

Austin sat straight up in his chair. His uncle's voice was chilling, and his eyes had turned ugly.

"Look at the choice she's made in this," Uncle Drayton said. "She's run off to live in some dog-trot house with a bunch of white trash."

"She's not living there, Drayton—"

"And they're not trash!" Austin cried. He stood up with a jolt, slamming his middle against the table. "I'm sorry, sir, but I don't think you know anything about it!"

"Sit down, Austin," Uncle Drayton said icily.

"Sir, I—"

"Sally, why didn't you and Wesley teach him some manners?"

Austin swallowed and pulled back his voice. "At least I'm not a hypocrite, sir."

Uncle Drayton drew himself up until Austin could barely see his eyes over his nose. "I beg your pardon, young man. I have enough trouble being called names by the secessionists. I will not have it from you."

"But are you any different from them?" Austin said.

"That's enough!"

"You don't want them forcing you to do things their way, but aren't you doing the same thing to Kady?"

"You know nothing about it!"

"But I do, sir. I was being a hypocrite, too."

"You are 11 years old!" Uncle Drayton looked around the table with his forehead puckered. "Why am I arguing with this boy?"

"Because he's struck a chord in you, Drayton," Mother said. "You must think about this before you go off hunting your own daughter down."

"He doesn't have to hunt me down," said a voice from the doorway. "I'm here."

✛ ⚜ ✛

Chapter Eighteen

Kady stood in the doorway looking pale and small in her black cape. Charlotte knocked over her chair getting to her. Everyone else sat as if they were frozen.

When Uncle Drayton finally stood up, Sally Hutchinson was on him like a pouncing cat.

"Think it through, Drayton," she said quietly. "This is your daughter."

"Leave us, all of you," he said in an icy voice.

"I want Aunt Sally to stay," Kady said. "I won't talk to you without her."

Uncle Drayton didn't answer but pushed through them all to the dining room door and crossed the hall with clicking heels. Kady latched on to Sally's arm and followed. Aunt Olivia bustled behind, muttering, "Why on earth did she wear that hideous cape? The whole parish will be talking!"

The library door closed behind the four of them with a slam that shuddered through Austin. It was all he could do not to hurl himself against it and plaster his ear to the keyhole.

"Well, what are we waiting for?" Polly said. "We can listen from under the stairs!"

Austin sucked in his breath. "We can't," he said. "I promised."

Polly rolled her eyes. "You and your hypocrites."

"What *do* we do?" Charlotte said. "I can't just sit here."

"Only one thing to do, far as I can tell," Henry-James said. "We got to go see Daddy 'Lias."

With Tot and Jefferson in tow, they made their way through the dank November night to Slave Street. Daddy Elias was rocking by the fire, and he had a surprise when they arrived.

A brown, baggy-skinned head rose from the floor, and a pair of droopy eyes shone in the firelight. A tail sleepily slapped the wood.

"Bogie!" Henry-James cried.

From deep in his floppy throat, Bogie answered. Henry-James flew to him and buried his face against his neck—and Austin was sure it was so the rest of them wouldn't see him cry. Austin felt a lump in his own throat. At least one thing was turning out right.

"It's a miracle!" Polly said as she hurried importantly to the shelves and brought down a pot for tea.

"You 'zactly right, Miz Polly," Daddy Elias said. "Ria, she done all she could, and then the onliest thing to do was pray. Jus' tonight when I come home, Bogie lif' up his head and start to sniffin'."

Austin got down on his knees beside Bogie and got a welcoming lick on the hand. "Narvel was right," he said. "I told you he wasn't all bad."

Charlotte nodded as she dug her fingers into the folds in Bogie's neck. Like all of them, her eyes were still sad.

"Look like we got some chilrun here wantin' another miracle," Daddy Elias said. His spoon-mouth softened.

Jefferson crawled into his lap, and Austin sank down next to Bogie.

"What's got these chins draggin' the ground?" the old man said.

"Kady's gonna get in trouble," Jefferson said. "She ran away and now Uncle Drayton's gonna punish her by making her marry that man with the red face."

"My mother'll stop him," Austin said, with more confidence than he felt.

Polly stopped pouring molasses over a piece of cornbread and shook her head at Austin. "Don't count on it," she said. "Daddy had that look on his face."

"But he's got a lot of good in him, Uncle Drayton does," Austin said. He stopped—he'd surprised even himself. But he couldn't throw stones at Uncle Drayton, not after what he'd found out about himself. He swallowed hard at the lump in his throat. "If we all pray like Daddy Elias did for Bogie, Uncle Drayton's good side will win."

Polly set the plate of cornbread-and-molasses in front of Daddy Elias and put her hands on her hips. "You won't catch me praying for Daddy after what he's done—threatening to drag Kady back by the hair."

Austin looked up at her, still stroking Bogie's head. "But didn't you ever get so mad at somebody you wanted to snatch them bald-headed or something?"

Polly sniffed. "A lady doesn't let anger overcome her."

"You must not be a lady, then," Charlotte said. "Just last month you pulled my nose practically off my face for saying you were skinny."

Tot nodded in agreement, and Polly glared at her. "That was when I was a mere child," she said. "Before I met Garrison and realized what it meant to be a true woman."

Charlotte made a face over Bogie's back.

Austin looked at Daddy Elias. "Isn't that true, Daddy Elias?" he said. "We shouldn't criticize somebody else unless we're perfect?"

Daddy Elias smiled the spoon-shaped smile. "You singin' a

different tune than you done before, Massa Austin," he said. "I think you done learned 'bout them stones."

"What stones?" Polly said.

But before anyone could answer, the cabin door flew open. In the November wind, a black cape swirled, filling the doorway.

No one said a word to Kady, at least not for the long moment she stood there, eyes sparkling, cheeks bright from running from the Big House. It was Austin, of course, who started the flood of questions.

"What happened?" he said.

"Is Daddy making you get married?" Charlotte asked.

"Are you running away again?" Polly said—hopefully.

"I'll take you back through the forest, Miz Kady," Henry-James said. "Don't you go walkin' out there by yourself no more. You gonna get killed sure 'nuff."

"The only reason for me to go into the forest now, Henry-James," Kady said, "is to pick blackberries."

"What do you mean?" Austin said.

Kady's pretty face broke into a smile that lit the room. "I don't have to marry Garrison McCloud—or anyone else I don't want to."

Charlotte scrambled up and ran to her. "Daddy said that?"

Kady nodded, beaming. "Thanks to Aunt Sally. If she hadn't been there, I would be walking down the aisle four days from now."

"Aunt Sally is my favorite aunt," Polly said.

"She's your only aunt," Charlotte said.

"And Uncle Drayton agreed to that?" Austin said.

Kady nodded, her face still surprised. "He said he only wants what's best for us. Aunt Sally said parents don't always know what that is, though—especially with things changing the way they are." Kady grinned. "She almost spoiled it when she told him he was acting like a hypocrite. He said he was sick of hearing that word."

"What did Mama say?" Charlotte said.

"Nothing. She isn't speaking to me."

"She'll come around," Polly said, "once she realizes she can use all her wedding preparations for me. I think that gown she had made for Kady will fit—"

"Henry-James!" a voice trumpeted from outside the cabin. "Boy, are you in there?"

"Yes, Marse!" Henry-James called out. He leaped over Bogie, but the door was flung open before he could take another step. Uncle Drayton smacked it shut behind him and flashed his eyes at Henry-James. The black boy seemed to shrivel even as Austin watched.

"Evenin', Marse Drayton," Daddy Elias said.

"I'm not here to pay a call, Elias," Uncle Drayton said. "I've come for this deceitful boy."

Henry-James's eyes went to the floor, and Bogie whined and struggled to get up.

"What I done, Marse Drayton?" Henry-James said.

"The worst possible thing you can do to your master besides run away," Uncle Drayton said through his teeth. "You lied to me."

Henry-James jerked his head up. "I ain't told you no lies, Marse Drayton. I swear!" His eyes went back to the floor, and he kept shaking his head. Austin wasn't sure whether he was denying or just trembling in fear. Austin's own heart was starting to slam.

"It isn't what you told me, boy," Uncle Drayton said tightly. "It's what you *didn't* tell me."

Austin looked quickly at Charlotte. Her freckles looked stark naked against her white face.

"You knew all along where Kady was hiding, yet you kept it from me."

"I promised Miz Kady I weren't gonna tell nobody!"

"Is Miss Kady your master?"

Henry-James shook his head miserably.

"Answer me!"

"Daddy, really, this isn't fair," Kady said.

"I've heard enough from you tonight, young lady!"

"Evidently not!" Kady's eyes gleamed anger. "You're still acting like a little boy who didn't get his own way!"

"Out!" Uncle Drayton cried. His tan face was crimson, his lips tight-white against his teeth. "All of you—out!"

"Daddy, come on. You've been so generous tonight. Why can't you just let this go, too?"

"I will handle my affairs without this constant contradiction! Go on, out of here!"

Polly ushered Tot and Charlotte out the door, and Kady followed angrily, holding Jefferson by the hand.

"What does deceitful mean?" Jefferson whispered loudly.

Austin started after them, his face burning and his mind shooting angry sparks. *Ask Uncle Drayton,* he wanted to shout. *He should know.*

He felt a firm hand on his shoulder.

"You stay, Austin," Uncle Drayton said. "Maybe what you're about to see will convince you that you don't do this boy any favors when you put ideas in his head."

"What am I about to see?" Austin said. His stomach began to churn.

"Henry-James, lean over that chair." Uncle Drayton reached inside his greatcoat and pulled out a leather strap fringed with long tails.

"You're not going to whip him, are you?" Austin said. His insides surged toward his throat. "It was my idea to follow the map.

Henry-James was just trying to protect Charlotte and me!"

"Then as far as I'm concerned, you should be whipped as well," Uncle Drayton said. "Since I can't do that, this boy can take your licks for you."

"No!" Austin cried. "Don't whip him, please!"

But Uncle Drayton shoved Henry-James's head down over the back of the chair with one hand and ripped open his shirt with the other.

He only gets two shirts a year! Austin thought wildly. *And you've gone and ripped one of them!*

The shirt was the least of it. Uncle Drayton lifted the hand that held the whip high over his head and with a snap of his wrist brought the nine-tails down across Henry-James's bare back. The black boy's spine arched up like a cat's, and a cry burst from him that went straight through Austin.

"Daddy Elias, make him stop!" Austin cried.

But the old man sat with his head bowed and his gnarled hands holding back a whimpering Bogie. Again the whip came down and slashed across the raw skin.

Austin made a jump for Uncle Drayton's arm. The whip snapped back, on its way to Henry-James once more. Its sharp tails cut into Austin's cheek—so hard that his head went backward and carried the rest of him with it. The floor smacked against his skull and sent the room spinning.

"Good heavens—Austin!" Uncle Drayton cried.

Austin heard the whip slap to the floorboards, felt firm hands on the sides of his face. He shook his head away and blinked his way back.

"Are you all right, son?" Uncle Drayton said. "Austin, are you hurt?"

"Don't whip him!" Austin said. His tongue was thick, his throat closing fast. "Didn't you ever tell a lie to protect somebody? Didn't you ever think you were right and everybody else was wrong?"

Uncle Drayton ran his hand gently along Austin's cheek. "You stepped right in my way. Your mother is going to have my hide."

"Didn't you?" Austin cried.

Uncle Drayton closed his eyes. "That's enough for tonight. Did you learn your lesson, boy?"

Henry-James straightened from the chair. Only Austin saw his eyes, and he shivered. They were stone-cold and hard with hate.

"Yes, Marse," Henry-James said. "I done learned."

Austin squirmed away from his uncle and slid backward to the wall. His chest was heaving, and he couldn't stop the words that burst from him.

"How about you, Uncle Drayton?" he cried. "Have you learned yours?"

"Austin, enough."

"I learned *mine!* I learned what a know-it-all, better-than-everybody-else person I am. I learned I can't be a hypocrite. I have to admit the stupid things I do. How come you can't learn that, Uncle Drayton?"

Uncle Drayton straightened up. Slowly, he picked up the cat-o'-nine-tails. Austin watched, heart hammering, as he tucked it back inside his greatcoat. He was at the door before he turned to Austin again.

"I do what I think is right," he said in a faraway voice. "There was a time when I always knew what that was."

With that he opened the door and left amid a windy tumble of leaves.

"I reckon you best go now, too, Massa Austin," Daddy Elias said. "Henry-James got to get the shame off'n his face 'fore he look at you again."

"Shame?" Austin said. "You don't have anything to be

ashamed of, Henry-James! Uncle Drayton's the one who ought to be ashamed!"

"I reckon Marse Drayton *is* 'shamed," Daddy Elias said. "I ain't never seen him hang his head like he jus' done."

Austin felt himself sag. "I'm so confused, Daddy 'Lias," he said. "I don't know what to think."

"You been learnin' 'bout that beam you got to get out your eye and them stones you ain't throwin' no more. Don't you be judgin' Marse Drayton. You jus' give him to Marse Jesus, and He gonna fix him right up."

"Who gonna fix *you* up, Massa Austin?" Henry-James said. He crawled over to Austin and pointed to his cheek. "You swellin' up like a chipmunk."

Austin put his hand up to feel his stinging wound, but a large, wet tongue got there first.

Henry-James scratched behind Bogie's ear as the dog licked Austin's face. "Well, I reckon that answer that question, don't it?"

Sally Hutchinson did not "have her brother's hide" when she saw Austin's face, but she did, as she put it, give him a "good-sized piece of her mind." After that, Austin held his breath, wondering if his mother's next sentence would be, "We're leaving tomorrow."

Mother's conversation with her brother was enough to keep Uncle Drayton from complaining when Kady began to spend more time than ever with her in the next few weeks. When she wasn't in her aunt's room talking, she was in some corner reading and, of course, writing poetry.

She'd been right, Austin observed. Aunt Olivia didn't speak a word to Kady for days. Only when Kady started expressing an interest in going to Charleston after Christmas did her mother soften up a little and begin making plans to convert the wedding gown into a ball dress. She even arranged for Kady to go to the city at once for French lessons.

It didn't look as if Polly were going to need a wedding gown anytime soon, at least not for Garrison McCloud. He didn't show his face at Canaan Grove again after the day Uncle Drayton told him the wedding was off. One afternoon, Austin found Polly in the music room, her head thrown down on top of the piano, sobbing into her ruffled sleeves.

"What's wrong?" Austin said. "Did the lid fall on your head?"

Polly glared at him out of swollen red eyes. "Get out if you're going to make fun of me," she said.

"I wasn't making fun of you. I thought you were hurt."

"I am! My heart is broken!"

"Garrison McCloud?"

She nodded miserably and dabbed at her eyes with a lace handkerchief she pulled out of her cuff. She hadn't quite trained Tot to be ready the way Mousie was.

"You promise not to laugh at me?" she said.

Austin nodded. "Who am I to laugh at somebody else? I've done some pretty silly things myself."

"I *have* been silly!" she cried. "I thought when Garrison paid so much attention to me when he was here that he really cared about me. Now I know he was just using me to make Kady jealous. She knew it, too, and she tried to protect me."

She began to cry anew. Austin shifted uncomfortably from foot to foot. "Sorry," he said.

"That doesn't help."

Austin was sure he didn't know what *would*. He looked longingly at the door and fumbled for some words. "Why would you want to marry that old Garrison McCloud anyway?" he said finally.

"Because he's handsome and rich and I thought he was wonderful."

"Wonderful?" Austin said. "He's nothing but a hypocrite."

Polly brought her head up and blinked at him. "What *is* that anyway?"

"It's somebody who says he believes one thing and then turns around and acts like something else. He pretended like he was such a gentleman, paying you all that attention, but . . . he wasn't . . ." Austin finished lamely.

Polly's eyes brightened for a moment, but her face puckered again. "It doesn't matter whether he was a hypocrite or not," she said miserably. "No one is ever going to pick me over Kady. I'm homely!"

Austin cocked his head at her. "You used to be," he said. "But lately, I haven't been thinking that so much."

She looked as if she didn't know whether to smack him or hug him. To Austin's relief, she didn't do either.

"You haven't?" she said. "Was it because of my hairpiece? Or my replacement teeth?"

"Replacement teeth?" Austin said. He leaned in and stared at her mouth as she smiled for him. "Hey, they aren't brown anymore!"

"Mama got me new ones when we came back from Flat Rock last summer, and then I got my hairpiece. And I tried so hard to learn to be a good plantation wife. But I'll still never get a husband—I know I won't!"

She threw herself down on top of the piano again, but this time the tears didn't bother Austin so much. He was too busy studying Polly and thinking scientifically.

"I don't think it was the hairpiece or the new teeth," he said after a minute of surveying her. "Although I'd like to learn how they did that—but I think you look better because I like you better."

She straightened up and dabbed uselessly at her face with the wet hanky.

"That doesn't make sense," she said.

"Yes, it does. Sometimes, when Uncle Drayton's treating everybody nice and being generous, I look at him and I think how handsome he is and how I want to look like him when I'm grown. But then when he's whipping Henry-James or yelling at Daddy Elias, I almost hate him and then I think he's the ugliest man who ever lived."

"Oh," Polly said. She stood there, looking something like a turtle who was deciding whether to go back into her shell or take a chance and keep her neck out. Finally, she stuck out her hand, palm down, and said, "Thank you, Austin. You might turn out to be something of a southern gentleman after all."

Austin stared blankly at her hand. "What's this for?"

"For you to kiss, silly," she said.

Austin felt his face going scarlet from the neck up. "I don't think I want to be *that* much of a gentleman," he said.

She rolled her eyes and flounced out of the music room. But Austin noticed that she didn't take her handkerchief with her.

In the weeks that followed, Uncle Drayton grew more and more quiet. He seldom smiled his charming smile or called them all by their pet names at the dinner table. Kady whispered to the children that he was waiting for a messenger to bring him an invitation to the convention regarding secession, but it didn't come. And she said every time there were hoofbeats on the drive, he was sure it was the Fire Eaters coming to throw him in jail.

When Kady returned from the city, she went back to giving Charlotte and Austin their lessons in the music room in the mornings and working with the slave children in the spring house in the afternoons. But the student she seemed most interested in was Henry-James. Whenever he wasn't working for Uncle Drayton, Kady had him huddled with her by a tree, talking and gesturing with her hands, her face alive and working hard.

Austin was dying to get in on one of those conversations. They looked like the beginning of an adventure to him. But Kady said they were just between Henry-James and her. One day, he and Charlotte found out why.

Henry-James was unusually quiet that early December evening as the three of them popped corn over the fire on Slave Street before Ria and Daddy Elias came in from the day's work.

Austin finally poked him in the ribs and said, "What's wrong, Henry-James? Cat got your tongue?"

Bogie sat up with interest and began sniffing for the cat in question, but Henry-James sadly shook his head. "Ain't no cat, Massa Austin," he said. "It's Miz Kady done got me keepin' secrets—and I don't like it."

"Secrets from who?" Charlotte said.

"About what?" Austin said.

Henry-James's eyes drooped toward the fire. "From you—'bout me. I feels like one o' them hypo-things you always goin' on 'bout, Massa Austin."

"Why doesn't she want you to tell us whatever it is?" Austin said.

Charlotte put her hand on Henry-James's arm. "You don't have to tell us," she said. "I haven't even heard what it is and I already don't like it."

"I gotta tell you!" Henry-James burst out. "You the onliest friends I got 'sides Bogie."

Austin stared hard at the toes of his boots. *More secrets*, he thought. *Secrets always mean more lies, more sneaking, more being a hypocrite. Are we ever gonna be done with this?*

He looked up to find Henry-James watching him closely, his lips pursed in waiting.

"I won't say nothin' 'less you wants me to, Massa Austin," he said. "You 'bout as close to Jesus as Daddy 'Lias—and if'n you says no, then I says no."

Austin's chest felt ready to break open. He looked helplessly at Henry-James and Charlotte. "The only thing I know," he said, "is that I don't know everything. I don't know whether to hear your secret or not, because if we have to lie again and sneak around and people get in trouble—"

"Then I'm gonna keep it to myself for now," Henry-James said decidedly. "And when we all knows the time is right, then it'll come spillin' on out."

"How will we know?" Charlotte said.

They both looked at Austin. He could only shrug. "We have to let Jesus do the thinking on that one," he said.

It was just a few days later when Austin was headed down the path to the pond to meet Charlotte. He was looking up, commenting to himself how naked the trees suddenly looked now that their leaves were all gone, when he spotted something red on one of the branches. It didn't take him more than a blink or two to figure out it was Narvel. Austin felt his eyes narrow. He stopped and folded his arms as he gazed upward.

"I hate to tell you this, Narvel," Austin said, "but that isn't a very good hiding place."

"I ain't hidin'," Narvel said. "I'm just gettin' the rest of my things."

"What things?"

Narvel stuck out a piece of rope.

"Oh," Austin said. He squinted at the tree. It *was* the one he'd hung by his ankle from, but it looked so different now. A lot of things did.

"So are you coming down?" Austin said.

"Depends," Narvel said.

"On what?"

"On whether you're gonna stand there and spit them big words at me."

"I should, you know. You shot Bogie—nearly killed him."

"Is he all right?"

"What do you care?" Austin said.

Narvel tilted his big head, and for the first time ever, Austin saw that straight line of a mouth crumple. He also saw that one of the usually mean, green eyes was blue-black and swollen shut.

"I wasn't the one shot that dog," Narvel said. "I wouldn't shoot nobody, man nor beast, 'less I was gonna eat it, or it done somethin' to me first."

"Who did it then?"

"My daddy. He took my gun and done it."

Narvel's head tilted down even farther. The black-and-blue eye made Austin wince.

"Was he the one who did that to your eye, too?" Austin said.

The big head just nodded. Austin felt himself nodding, too. It wasn't much different from Uncle Drayton taking a whip to Henry-James. That shouldn't happen to any boy.

Austin rubbed the back of his neck, which was starting to ache from looking up in the tree for so long, and said, "Thanks for giving Kady a place to stay."

Narvel shrugged. "It wasn't nothin'."

Austin shrugged, too. "I have to go."

He started off down the path.

"You gonna meet one of your friends?" Narvel said.

"Yes."

Narvel poked at the end of his rope with his finger. "Guess you better go on then."

Austin could still see him in his head as he walked on. Nobody, he decided, who looked that utterly sad could be as bad as Narvel tried to be. And Austin was glad.

So many things are solved now, Austin prayed later as he lay in bed with a hot brick near his feet. *Kady doesn't have to marry Garrison. Polly isn't such a snake-child anymore. Narvel is leaving Henry-James alone, Bogie is well, and I'm not Mr. Know-it-all.*

He churned restlessly. *But Jesus, I sure wish I did know everything—like whether to hear one more secret—and what's gonna happen to Uncle Drayton if the South secedes—and when Father is coming for us.*

He stopped praying and sat up in his bed, because he couldn't lie still any longer. His mother had written the letter—he'd seen it himself. Every time the mail came, Austin waited with his breath held, but so far there had been no reply.

He threw back the covers and padded across the bare floor. So many things seemed unsure. When something was certain in his head, he had to do something about it.

His mother was still up, curled in a brocade chair and looking listless and little-girlish. She smiled faintly when he came in.

"You couldn't sleep either?" she said.

"I don't want to go back north with Father yet," Austin blurted out. "It doesn't feel right. I don't think Jesus *wants* us to go now."

Mother patted the floor by the chair with her foot, and Austin sank gratefully onto the spot. She ran her hand over his mussed-up hair.

"I've been sitting here thinking about that very thing," she said. "I've been thinking that I don't want to go either, but I couldn't find a reason why. There's every reason to leave, you know."

Austin opened his mouth to protest, but she put a frail finger on his mouth. "Things are so unsettled in the South. Uncle Drayton is struggling like a drowning man. Aunt Olivia would pack our bags for us if we decided to go. I'm certainly well enough to travel." She gave a brisk little sigh. "But I don't feel right about leaving either and I don't know why—or at least I didn't, until you just told me."

Austin looked up at her quickly, and she folded her hands in her nightgown-lap. He said, "We don't always have to have a reason, do we? I mean, everything doesn't have to be scientifically proven. If you believe that, then I'm certainly convinced!"

She grinned, and her sad eyes danced a little. "When we have God, we don't always need a reason. It's when we start thinking we have all the answers that we make mistakes."

Austin nodded solemnly. "But what about your letter to Father? Do you have to write to him again? What if he's already on his way here?"

"I don't see why he would be," Mother said. Still smiling, she picked up the Bible on the table and reached inside the cover, drawing out an envelope. "I never sent it. And I could never figure out why."

Austin felt his first grin in days. "Can I tear it up?" he said.

She shook her head. "No, but you can burn it. And I promise you I won't write another one like it until we both know for sure it's time to go."

Austin took the letter from her and looked to the fireplace.

"Go ahead," she said. "It's all right."

So Austin poked the letter into the flames, and they both sat watching as it crinkled into soft ashes.

"You know something, Austin?" she said. "I think Jesus might accomplish the impossible after all."

There's More Adventure in the
CHRISTIAN HERITAGE SERIES!

The Salem Years, 1689–1691

The Rescue #1

Josiah and his older sister, Hope, used to fight a lot. But now, she's very sick. And neither the town doctor nor all the family's wishing can save her. Their only earthly chance is an old widow—a stranger to Salem Village—whose very presence could destroy the family's relationship with everyone else! Can she save Hope? And at what price?

The Stowaway #2

Josiah is going to town! Sent to Salem Town to be educated, Josiah Hutchinson's dream of someday becoming a sailor now seems within reach. But a tough orphan named Simon has other plans, and his evil schemes could get both Josiah and Hope in a heap of trouble. How will the kids prove their innocence? Whose story will the village believe?

The Guardian #3

Josiah has heard the wolves howling at night, and he's devised a way of dealing with them. But with the perfect night to execute the plan approaching, there's still one not-so-small problem—Cousin Rebecca, who follows Josiah around like his shadow ... even into danger! How will Josiah protect her? What will happen to the wolves?

The Accused #4

Josiah Hutchinson is robbed by the cruel Putnam brothers! In a desperate attempt to retrieve his stolen property, he's accused of being the thief and unexpectedly finds himself on trial for crimes he didn't commit! Can Josiah find the courage to tell the truth? Will anyone believe him if he does? Will he be torn from his family and locked away in a dingy jail cell?

The Samaritan #5

Taking to heart a message he heard at church, Josiah attempts to help a starving old widow and her daughter. But while he's trying hard to forge new friendships, the feud with the Putnams is getting out of control. Will Josiah be clever enough to escape their wicked ways? Can God protect him when it seems hopeless?

The Secret #6

Hope's got a crush on someone—and Josiah knows who it is! Can he keep it a secret? After all, if Papa found out who she's been sneaking away to see, he'd be furious! And if the Putnams find out, who knows what will happen!

The Williamsburg Years, 1780–1781

The Rebel #1

The Hutchinson family history continues in the first book of the Williamsburg Years. Josiah's great-grandson, Thomas, doesn't think he'll ever like Williamsburg. Things get worse when the apothecary shop he works in is robbed! Thomas thinks he knows who did it, but before he can prove it, he's accused of the crime and taken to jail. How will he convince everyone he's innocent?

The Thief #2

Horses are being stolen in Williamsburg! And after Thomas sees a masked rider leading a horse, he believes it's Nicholas, the new doctor who has come to town. When Thomas's friend is seriously injured, Thomas knows the young doctor may be his friend's only chance. Can he trust Nicholas to take care of him?

The Burden #3

Thomas Hutchinson knows secrets, but he can't tell them to anyone! And he soon learns that "bearing one another's burdens," as he heard in church, is not always easy—especially when a crazed Walter Clark holds him at gunpoint for a secret he doesn't even know! Will Walter ever believe Thomas? How will he be freed of these secrets?

The Prisoner #4

War in Williamsburg is raging! But when Thomas's mentor, Nicholas, refuses to fight, he is carried off against his will by the Patriots. Witnessing this harsh treatment, Thomas feels confused and trapped. Whose side should he be on? Will he ever understand what it means to be free?

The Invasion #5

When word arrives that Benedict Arnold and his men are ransacking plantations nearby, Thomas, his family, and friends return to their homestead to protect it. But British soldiers break in, taking food, horses, and Caroline as hostage! Now what? Will Thomas be able to help straighten out this horrible situation?

The Battle #6

Though the war is all around him, Thomas is more frustrated by the *internal* fighting he feels. He's expected to take orders from a woman he doesn't like, he's forbidden to talk about his missing brother, Sam, and, to top it all off, he's not getting along with two of his closest friends. Will nothing turn out right?

The Charleston Years, 1860–1861

The Misfit #1

When the crusade to abolish slavery reaches full swing,

Austin Hutchinson (Thomas's great-grandson) is sent to live with relatives. But he's not sure he'll enjoy his stay because his cousins—Kady, Polly, and Charlotte—don't seem to like him. Even Henry-James, the slave boy, wants nothing to do with him. Will Austin ever find his place?

The Ally #2

When Austin discovers that Henry-James can't read, Austin resolves to teach him—even though it's illegal to educate slaves. But that only leads to trouble! Uncle Drayton is furious when he realizes Henry-James has secretly been given lessons and locks him in an old shack until he can be sold. Can Austin free Henry-James without getting them into more trouble? Will he able to forgive Uncle Drayton for being so harsh?

The Threat #3

Trouble has a way of following Austin wherever he goes! First, while traveling to the Ravenals' vacation home, he overhears two men scheming against his Uncle Drayton and spies a lanky boy tampering with the family's stagecoach. Then, while playing one afternoon near the church, Austin and Charlotte have a run-in with the same boy and his brother! Can Austin find peace amidst all the hostility?

Available at a Christian bookstore near you